Dark Justice

Portia of the Pacific Historical Mysteries

Volume 5

JAMES MUSGRAVE

ISBN: 978-1-943457-40-3

Published by EMRE Publishing Fiction
San Diego, CA

Dark Justice

By

James Musgrave

© 2020 by James Musgrave

Published by English Majors, Reviewers and Editors, LLC

An English Majors, Reviewers and Editors Book Copyright 2020

English Majors, Reviewers and Editors Publishers is a publishing house based in San Diego, California.

Website: emrepublishing.com

For more information, please contact:

English Majors, Reviewers and Editors, LLC

DEDICATION

To women, who deserve our utmost respect and appreciation. At the very least, they have the right to determine their destiny, which includes life and death decisions about what they can do with their bodies.

Other Works by This Author

Forevermore: A Pat O'Malley Historical Mystery
Disappearance at Mount Sinai: A Pat O'Malley Historical Mystery
Jane the Grabber: A Pat O'Malley Steampunk Mystery
Steam City Pirates: A Pat O'Malley Steampunk Mystery
The Digital Scribe: A Writer's Guide to Electronic Media
Lucifer's Wedding
Sins of Darkness
Russian Wolves
Iron Maiden an Alternate History
Love Zombies of San Diego
Freak Story: 1967-1969
Catalina Ghost Stories

Portia of the Pacific Historical Mysteries
Chinawoman's Chance
The Spiritualist Murders
The Stockton Insane Asylum Murder
Portia of the Pacific Historical Mystery Trilogy
The Angel's Trumpet

Interactive and Multimedia Enhanced eBooks

EMRE Publishing is now selling completely "enhanced" versions of its books through the unique Embellisher Multimedia Stream platform. Simply register inside the eReader to have access to the variety of titles. They contain relevant historical videos, music, interactive content, and a complete audiobook edition in many of the great titles.

Visit https://emrepublishing.com/new_embellisher-ereader/ to see what's available. Enter your email and a password to register and view. Buy your future digital copies of this Portia of the Pacific Historical Mystery series at reduced prices here: https://books.bookfunnel.com/portiaofpacific

"Abortion isn't a lesser evil, it's a crime. Taking one life to save another. That's what the Mafia does. It's a crime. It's an absolute evil."
—Pope Francis

"Looking through the bent-backed tulips
To see how the other half live
Looking through a glass onion."
—The Beatles, "Glass Onion"

"Sit and drink pennyroyal tea. I'm anemic royalty."
—Kurt Cobain, "Pennyroyal Tea" from Nirvana's *In Utero*.

Table of Contents

Chapter 1: Journal Found in the Park

San Francisco California, Golden Gate Park, June 20, 1887.

My name is Penelope Farmer. I am on my way to the clinic in Chinatown when I see the head of a crow. At first, I think it might be a voodoo doll, or charred food. It is lying on the path in front of one of the long benches in Golden Gate Park. I bend over to see it better. I can see the pitch-black head feathers, shiny with oil; the single eye, a milky film on its black pupil; the smoky-gray beak, opened slightly, as if the head has been lopped off mid-caw; no blood, no gore; just a warning message from one of my mother's Navajo dreams.

My mother, Haseya, which means "she rises," in the Navajo tongue, has been dead for three years. I was eleven at the funeral. I remember my mother teaching me about the power of dreams and tribal destiny. But my father says I need to learn to be a True Woman, without the superstitions and ghastly visions of my Native heritage. He appoints a private tutor, Mrs. Althea Crutchfield, who teaches me the basic skills of reading and math required for the True Woman of wealth. "Due to her emotional and physical frailty, a True Woman," according to Mrs. Crutchfield, "needs to be protected by a male family member. She is not supposed to think on her own, as that is the role of her protector and the other men of the Great Society."

Three years before my mother dies, when I am eight, my father is full of attentive love. He takes mother and I to all the best stores in San Francisco. He praises my progress in my lessons and buys me all the books I ask him to get me. He even takes us on a trip to Arizona territory, where father and mother first met on the reservation, and where my mother sold blankets and hand-crafted jewelry in the tribal store. That is when my mother first began to cough up blood, and I met her tribal medicine man. His name was Hástin Yázhe. He was tall, and he wore strange clothing. There was a young woman, also wearing native dress, who followed him all around, as if she were his shadow. He told me her name was Ajei and that she was a mute.

Shortly after the doctor in San Francisco says my mother has contracted consumption, our medicine man appears at our door. He says he has medicine to help us both. He tells Mrs. Crutchfield to give it to us both from now on, three times a day, after our meals. Mrs. Crutchfield was a nurse at one of the orphanage schools in which she taught, so she knows how to give us the three injections each day. My mother and I feel much better.

My mother even has a dream that first night we started our Navajo medicine. She sleeps beneath the Dream Catcher to prevent bad dreams. She says her husband, my father, Aloysius, is going to change. The week after this dream, she and I are working in the garden, and we see a coyote wandering on California Street next to our Nob Hill home. My mother screams and runs back into the house. But I stay, and I watch, entranced, as the ghostly gray cur begins to walk on his hind legs and then takes off, at great speed, running down the hill like a human. That same night my father begins to beat my mother after she fails to pay him proper respect. She screams and curses at him in Navajo, something she has never done before. I know she is dying, and she takes out all her anger and fear on him.

But one year later, on the night of a full moon, as I pull mother's body up on the pillow, I can feel her ribs under the night dress, and her breathing is a constant wheezing. Just as the moon radiates through the bedroom window upon her thin face, I see the long snout and white fangs of the coyote. My mother has transformed her voice into yips and yaps. That's when she first tells me about *yee naaldooshii*, the skinwalker we saw the week before in the front yard. We were both too afraid to speak of it until now. She tells me this creature is the tribal witch who can take the form of an animal and haunt a person who is inflicting harm upon someone in our tribe. As a result, Navajo Holy People wear only two animal skins, the sheepskin and the buckskin, and then only for ceremonial purposes. When I ask her into which animals the skinwalker can change, my mother says that it is usually a coyote, owl, fox, wolf or crow--although a skinwalker witch does have the ability to turn into any animal she chooses.

On the second night after the full moon, just before my mother dies of consumption, she asks me, her eleven-year-old daughter, to come close to the bed. When my mother moves her hand and brings it to her lips, I know she wants to whisper something, so I lean forward and I can feel her thin fingers form a circle around her lips against my ear. "I am *yee naaldooshii*," she says, yipping and spraying saliva. "And so are you," she whispers. The final vowels become a howling echo, and then my mother dies.

Three years later, when I am fourteen, my father begins to visit me at night. Outside, I can hear the coyote howl, and I begin to create my own myth, my personal Navajo legend. I am transformed into my mother, taking her place, and what father starts to do to me is because I am now possessed by the spirit of Haseya. During the day, as I do the chores, go shopping, instruct the mansion staff, everything, I do it just as mother did. And, in the bedroom at night, I can feel his probing hands, his great weight, his sweaty skin, and his kisses. I can hear his whispers of affection, his grunting, and can watch, with fascination, at the rising tumor below his waist. I am Haseya. One night, I bleed on the sheets for the first time. When he leaves, I stand at the bay window in my mother's night dress and howl at the coyote standing alone outside in the foggy San Francisco night. Perhaps I am not the *yee naaldooshii*, the skinwalker. I am protecting my father from the tribal curse.

Two years pass, and when I stop having my monthlies, at age sixteen, I am afraid to tell my tutor, Mrs. Crutchfield. She might take me off my Navajo medicine. Thereafter, the City Library becomes my only escape. Kind Mrs. McMillan, the Head Librarian, shows me all the books I need to learn about my body and how it functions. After I learn I am pregnant, I know I need to act, before it is too late. I start to read the newspapers. Among all my father's ads for female patent medicines, are other ads; they tell women about places to go where their "menses problems" can be addressed in person. Magic words like "vagina," "uterus," "umbilical cord," "placenta," and "still birth" fill my dreams, complete with the drawings from the books.

At first, I admit, I want to poison or hang myself. Killing myself seems to be the only solution. I am too ashamed to approach anyone about what is happening with my father. I read the articles about other girls and women in my same predicament; they break the laws, use abortifacients such as father sells, and then they become prostitutes. Often, they die at the hands of women like Madame Restell, in New York City, who is called the "Abortionist Vampire." The female abortionist's image in the *Police Gazette* is especially dreadful. Below Restell's haunting figure is a flying vampire, a baby held in its clenched jaws. In the article, the author quotes from Lord Byron's poem, *The Giaour*:

> "Thy victims ere they yet expire
> Shall know thy demon for their sire,
> As cursing thee, thou cursing them,
> Thy flowers are withered on the stem."

I am terrified of meeting such a person. Is she another kind of *yee naaldooshii?* Yet, after week fifteen, I become more horrified of my future than I am of my present.

I read other magazines, such as the *Woodhull and Claflin Weekly*, and *Revolution*, the Women's Suffrage magazine. The articles explain domestic incest, voluntary motherhood, rape, and the prosecution of women who have no legal rights. Men and parents can place their pregnant daughters into insane asylums, or imprison them in private hospitals, or force them to give birth and then steal the child from the mother, selling it on the open market through agencies. Church organizations can use these bastard children, as working slaves, inside orphanages.

These magazines understand my problem, so I call and make the appointment with Mrs. Honora Fulbright, a midwife. Fulbright advertises in one of the women's magazines, and she is the woman who is performing the procedure today. Mrs. Fulbright charges what I can afford, so I steal the money from my father.

Today, I am mentally distraught, and my Navajo medicine is making me see things. Finding this crow's head is especially macabre. As I am also an amateur ornithologist, I know about crows and their "murders." I know how crows track each other; like women, they form covens in which they share their experiences in a complex process of interpersonal communications. If one is injured on the ground, the entire murder will fly over its body, circling and cawing maniacally, until there are enough of them, and then they will land near their wounded comrade. They will watch after, protect, and feed the incapacitated one, sometimes for weeks, and their animosity toward approaching enemies is cunning and vengeful.

I realize that this crow's head is a spirit sign, from my dead mother, for me to meditate upon. A human enemy has done this, and crows remember their enemies. I also know the crow can be a *yee naaldooshii,* a skinwalker.

I sit down on the park bench, my ruffled blue dress blowing haphazardly in the ocean's winds. As I stoop over to view the crow's head, my small straw hat, with the thin elastic chin band, snaps off, and rises from my black hair, upward, floating toward the cumulus puffs high in the cobalt sky.

I stare down at the crow's head, and I close my eyes; in my vision, my body replaces the crow on the ground the same way I replaced my mother. Except, in my vision, I have no head, only a torso, arms and legs. From my dreamer omniscience, I look up. Flying around in concentric circles, instead of crows, are other women, and my body is in the center. Each woman is a personification of the different stages in a pregnancy. The ones, like me, at fifteen weeks, have small bumps protruding at their midsections. Others, if they are pregnant for the first time, begin to show that bump later, as their stomach muscles have yet to become stretched from previous births. Still other women are larger, each one soaring above, like a gigantic child's balloon, her stomach displaying the harbinger of future life, budding inside her womb, like the Truth itself.

The flying women disappear, and my father, Aloysius, appears next. He is outside, in the garden, on Nob Hill. He never stands in the garden. There is a murder of crows flying just above his head. He reaches up, snatches one of the crows out of the air, and pulls it down to him. He yanks a knife from the sheath at his belt and holds the blade next to the squirming crow's neck. He stands, great and tall in his black top hat, tuxedo, and gleaming spats; he slices the head off the struggling crow; the head falls to earth, splattering speckles of blood on his white ankle covers; he curses and carries the crow's blood-spewing body inside the house. He walks resolutely over to the iron cauldron inside the pantry and drops it into the roiling water. This is where he makes his Dr. Goody's Female Menstrual Potions.

***

"Something's gone terribly wrong!" the girl screams.

Mrs. Fulbright stands at the end of the barber's chair in the kitchen, the metal probe in her gloved hands, her two children screaming next-door in the parlor.

The heroin tablets are working. The girl stares, in a mesmerized fog, down at the bloody sheet, which covers the lower half of her body. Her legs are spread wide apart, held in stirrups, and the blood is quickly soaking the sheet and the mattress beneath it.

The Chinese midwife doesn't know what to do. Her supervisor, Dr. Liu Wei, comes into the room from next-door. He frowns and turns toward her. The look on his face is both concerned and angry.

"What are you doing? Who is this child?" Dr. Liu Wei says.

They both watch the girl as she spreads her arms out, like a bird of prey, and screams, "My father, Aloysius Xavier Farmer, did this to me! He has impregnated his only daughter. I am not my mother. It is I, Penelope Farmer, and my death must be avenged!"

Chapter 2: Honor Lost

The Toy Mansion, Fifteen Nob Hill, San Francisco, June 23, 1887.

Trella Evelyn was home from college. She was reading in the library when the chimes told her somebody was at the front door of their new home. Mrs. Mary Hopkins, who had allowed them to stay with her at One Nob Hill for three years, had now become too demented to maintain her household. Her deceased husband's attorneys had taken over the mansion and forced all non-family members to find other accommodations.

Ah Toy, with a loan from her Uncle Pete, was able to purchase the new home at a reasonable price. They decided to save as much as they could, however, so while Trella and her four siblings were home for the summer, they would take turns doing the duties which would have normally fallen to the mansion's staff. Their grandparents, Elias and Talitha Shortridge, had moved back to San Jose.

Trella knew that most of the family was now part of their mother's detective and legal business, and Clara's new office was on the second floor. She and her siblings did not find the added encumbrance of acting as butlers, cooks, chauffeurs, and dish washers too demanding. In point of fact, they all wanted the chance to be part of any new case that might arise, as their mother's previous four cases were quite challenging.

As Trella walked out of the library, into the parlor, toward the front door, she adjusted the new green silk belt around her thin waist and tucked a lock of reddish-brown hair into her matching hair band. She was now taking courses in Drama at Berkeley, and she wore a bare-shouldered, green Taffeta frock that First Lady Frances Cleveland had made so popular. She had a great affinity with Mrs. Cleveland, as they were both twenty-one, and they shared many of the same values about Women's Rights and the fair treatment of Negroes.

Her brother, seventeen-year-old David Milton, who was kidnapped during their mother's most recent case in Washington D.

C., had an impeccable taste in female attire, and he helped her select it. Since he was now allowed to wear dresses around the mansion, Trella trusted Dr. McFarland, the family alienist's modern approach to her brother's psychological well being.

The chubby man standing on the front porch was a stranger. He wore a gentleman's brown derby, a matching extra-large corduroy suit, white shirt, and red silk necktie, and his shoes were the latest spats or gaiters from England. He spoke in an erudite manner, as he brought his right hand up to his derby's brim to salute her.

"Good morning, madam. Is this the residence of Mrs. Clara Shortridge Foltz, Attorney-at-Law? My name is Aloysius Xavier Farmer. I would like to speak with her concerning an important legal matter."

Trella smiled. She knew her mother would be pleased at the prospect of a new client. Without the largesse of Mrs. Hopkins, most of her money now had to be earned from her law practice. The detective side of things would have to wait.

"Why certainly, Mr. Farmer. Please come in. I can go up and inform my mother. I don't believe she is occupied at present." She waved the portly gentleman into the foyer, where she took his hat and hung it on the mahogany rack in the corner.

"Your place is very similar to my own. I live up the road at Twelve Nob Hill. Perhaps we had the same architect?"

Trella watched, as Mr. Farmer's eyes scanned the parlor. Ah Toy's art collection, both paintings and sculptures, covered the walls and filled a variety of strategically positioned *Feng Shui* locations. They accented the Oriental furniture: sofas, lamps, tables, and chairs.

The sunshine was streaming into the room from the bay window, as the red drapes were pulled back. Farmer nodded and began to strut around the room, taking in the décor. She watched, as his eyebrows rose with his wrinkled forehead, and he took in the view. His voluminous frame and ruddy facial features reminded her of John Bunny, the stage actor and comedian. He had recently appeared at Berkeley's campus theater as Fallstaff in *The Merry*

Wives of Windsor. Farmer's wide mouth, rather bulbous and veined nose, and three chins made her smile, remembering Fallstaff's antics. His lamb chop sideburns were dark-brown, the same color as his neatly parted, rather wispy hair. She guessed he was in his early forties.

"Did you live in China?" Mr. Farmer inquired, holding up a Ming vase and studying its blue dragon design.

"No. We have friends who came from China. The owner of this house, in fact, collects art and creates it as well. I shall go up to tell mother you're here. Please make yourself comfortable."

He nodded at her, and she turned around and walked over to the stairs. She noticed the morning's *Chronicle* lying on the small table next to the balustrade. The headline read: *Aloysius Farmer, the Abortifacient King, Sued!* So that's why he was looking for legal assistance. She picked up the paper, tucked it under her arm, and proceeded up the stairs.

Clara's office door was open. Trella tossed the newspaper onto her desk. "He's downstairs. Do you believe it proper to aid such a scandalous bounder? We don't need money *that* badly, do we?"

Her mother turned from her typewriter to glance at what she dropped on the desk. Noting the front page headline, she picked up the paper and began to read the story.

"As I've always taught you, my dear, prejudgement is the root word for prejudice. Once a mind has made a conclusion based upon rumor or even from personal experience, the path toward finding the real truth has been obstructed."

"Yes, mother. But your poor women's abortionist is both fat and sassy. He is downstairs waiting for your unbiased wisdom. I'm afraid I have already prejudged him as being Fallstaff, but you know how I can become overly dramatic. I shall never learn how to become the cold and calculating lawyer, I am afraid. Like you and Laura."

Clara looked up from the newspaper. Her eyes were clear and hazel blue, and she was wearing her usual formal attire, a navy ruffled affair, her neck buttoned up to her chin with a cameo, her auburn hair wound up in an old woman's Victorian coiffure, plumping out in the back like the large bustle she wore beneath her dress when working.

Trella waited. Clara finally looked up again.

"The gentleman is being sued by representatives of eighty various public and private groups, headed by the San Francisco Protestant Orphan Asylum, the first such establishment on the Pacific Coast, founded in 1851. It states that the plaintiffs are seeking damages of two hundred fifty thousand dollars. The charges are undisclosed."

"Now I see why you're interested," Trella said, scowling down at Clara. "But why not be on the accusing side of things?"

"The facts are that Mr. Farmer's daughter, who happens to be of half-Navajo heritage, named her father as the sire of her baby, before she tragically expired inside the residential clinic of Chinatown midwife, Mrs. Honora Fulbright. Under the law, because death bed statements are held to be true statements, Mr. Farmer has been named the father. Furthermore, as we in this suffragist household are quite aware, women and children are still considered chattel under our present laws."

"I know. Property. Can't vote. Can't make a contract or own property. Continue." Her sarcasm was purposeful, as the gentleman downstairs was probably capsizing Ah Toy's artwork with his stomach.

"The result is that the midwife has been arrested for manslaughter, and, because of the deathbed statement, Mr. Farmer's business is now in jeopardy. I shall now go down to discuss this further with our possible client. Please precede me, Trella, I need to make a case file for him."

"A case file? How can you be so certain he will accept? Also, why are you accepting *him*? His daughter was sixteen. She's dead. He raped her." She crossed her chest with her fists. "Would you represent a man who raped me? Just because he had a fortune?"

"Once more, you jump to awkward and inappropriate analogies. Each case has its own facts and its own human actors. These must be applied to the laws we have and not to the laws we think we should have. I shall meet you downstairs."

Trella was seated on the fringed red sofa with the giant golden dragon decorating the back. When Clara came down the stairs, she watched Mr. Farmer, who was wedged into one of the broad-backed yellow chairs near the fireplace, rise to a standing position with great difficulty.

Clara, she knew, would be all business, and she was. She shook his hand forcefully, the new case folder clutched under her left arm.

"Mr. Farmer, I am so sorry for your loss. It is times like these that family becomes a steady rock of support. I trust yours is assisting you to weather the emotional difficulties these incidents can bring? Please, let's go into the library, where I can take notes, and you can bring forth some clarity about what you might need."

"Certainly," he said, and they both began to walk toward the library, on the right, at the far end of the parlor.

The door chimes rang. Trella nodded to her mother. "I shall answer it," she said, rushing toward the front door.

This time it was the familiar face of her mother's partner and personal friend, Laura de Force Gordon. As usual, she wore what she termed her "lawyer for the people" uniform. A black dress, no bustle, with a gray bowed neckerchief, no hat, and black boots. She was eleven years her mother's senior, at forty-nine, yet her clothing was more suitable to an undertaker's matron, Trella thought, as she waved her inside.

"Trella, you won't believe who came to my office this morning," she began, striding into the parlor. "I am going to defend one of the most strident suffragettes in this community. As you may be aware, Mrs. Honora Fulbright assists women who have chosen to end an unwanted pregnancy. As it so happens, I believe in the right of a woman to choose when to bring a child into this world, as the community and the husband should not hold power over the female anatomy, especially when it concerns the woman's health, safety, privacy and financial instability."

"That is quite the coincidence, you see, because mother is presently in private consultation with the wealthy rapist who caused your Mrs. Fulbright to be accused of manslaughter." She smiled.

"Although the word, I would wager, could best be termed womanslaughter. Of course, under the law, do we also include the fetus as a victim? If that's the case, then we need to know its gender as well, do we not? The newspaper said the teenaged victim and would-be mother's name is Penelope Farmer. I trust she might be the Grimm's Fairy Tale version of all those farmer's daughter jokes, no?" She chuckled.

Laura frowned. "I'm afraid Clara may be right about your sarcastic manners. You will never make a decent lawyer if you presume that attitude."

She walked over to the dragon sofa and sat down. She patted the cushion next to her. "Please, attorney Gordon. Be seated. I shall cease and desist my sarcastic demeanor. Tell me about your new case."

Laura smiled and joined her. "I am also a dramatist, believe it or not, and I try to follow the Bard's proclamation about the world being a stage. You are probably stating what our public is now thinking, so I shall take your criticisms as representative of what will, most likely, soon be coming at me in the form of uneducated invective."

"Yes. But not with the cultured vocabulary that you are using," she pointed out. "Your client will be called a baby killer and murderess. And you? Perhaps the Devil's own attorney sent to defend her?"

It was Laura's turn to chuckle, but her lips remained firm. "I don't mean to haggle, but I would assume your critique extends to your mother. She is about to defend the living Satan in this case, is she not?"

She nodded. "Yes. I was already chastised for my critique, but my value seems to be in becoming what you attorneys call a 'devil's advocate,' so perhaps there is some salvation for me yet. Please continue with the armchair defense of this new client of yours."

"I cannot tell you much, as my attorney-client privilege is presently in effect. All I have is the police report and a personal journal found on a bench in Golden Gate Park that is allegedly written by the deceased victim, Penelope Farmer. However, since the press has already been buzzing around the facts at hand, I can tell you my more general stratagem." Laura pushed a lock of black hair from her forehead.

Trella envied the woman's impetuousness. She was so unlike her mother, who used her feminine wiles to throw the opponent off-guard. Laura came at her opposition like a bull defending his herd.

"Let me hear your plan. I am certain you have an excellent one," she said.

"As you and I know, the criminal justice system has made the act of aborting a fetus a crime, but not many cases have been pursued beyond manslaughter because of the very difficult *mens rea* of deliberate intent that must be proved. However, this case has been chosen as a cause celebre for the American Medical Association. Thus, according to the newspapers, I shall be contending with a professional witness. Dr. Horatio Storer will be the State's leading expert." Laura scowled. "Not only must I defend Mrs. Fulbright's actions in order to prove that Miss Farmer died from a spontaneous miscarriage that caused hemorrhaging, and not from Fulbright's negligence, I must also address Dr. Storer's accusations that any type of abortion is placing *any* pregnant female's life in immediate danger."

"I know you and mother differ on this. Whereas you are a socialist who believes in the collective rights of women to choose to have an abortion, mother tends to side with other suffragists, like Mrs. Anthony and Mrs. Stanton. They believe the act of abortion to be a mortal sin, and that one must first address the problems of women's rights and poverty before allowing prostitutes and other poor women to place their bodies at risk simply because they may be inconvenienced. Many suffragists say women die at the rate of thirty percent from surgeries and abortifacients." She was estimating her facts from what her mother had told her, but she wanted to play the good advocate.

"Don't you see? That's the point. I plan to refute this plan of the prosecution to make the case about morality and sin. Our

Constitution freed the slaves because they were deprived of their rights. Women, of all races, were not given that same privilege. If they put Storer on the stand to advocate his plan to force women to have all their children in his hospitals, then I shall rebut him by showing how forcing women to have children is a violation of personal privacy. Women, as citizens, should have the same constitutional protection as men and freed male slaves under the Fourteenth Amendment. The State, by forcing women to have children, is depriving them, without any trial, from having a chance at a healthy life, the liberty to freely choose when and with whom they can become pregnant, and the personal property that they might have earned had they not been forced to stay at home in order to raise these children."

She knew her mother's favorite rebuttal to this argument, so she decided to use it.

"However, the abortionist is often a profiteering scoundrel. Remember Madame Restell, in New York City? Since many of her clientele were from the privileged class, often married to Wall Street tycoons and other merchants, she would use the privacy issue to her advantage. She secured many so-called 'loans' from former patients, which were never returned. This amounted to nothing less than blackmail."

Laura nodded, but her frown showed she was ready with a rejoinder.

"Again, you have your mother's naivety in these matters. I contend that it is the very illegality of abortion which makes the practice susceptible to avarice. If we allow men in the medical profession, the so-called 'regulars,' like Dr. Storer, to gain control over women's reproductive rights, then the greedy exploiters like Restell will thrive. Only when women have legal control over their wombs will justice ever be served!" Laura raised her fist in the air.

"But what is your societal argument for this grand defense of women's rights?" She leaned forward in suspense. She knew this was Laura's first-ever case concerning this controversial topic.

"Thank you for asking. Before the industrialization of America, in the Seventeenth and Eighteenth Centuries, women took

21

care of family planning legally, in their own ways. Men did not intervene because women were protected by a wider support group of other women. When the cities began to isolate and separate men and women, these protections of privacy and female support fell apart, and women began to be exploited—both at work and in the bedroom. I therefore contend that the pregnant woman of today has become a victim of both the mental pressure of industrial growth and the wanton greed of male lust. These males have now turned on their women to force them into pregnancies that they cannot afford because of their legal and economic isolation and victimization."

Trella stood up. Her mother was coming out of the library with her new client, Mr. Farmer. She was smiling and nodding her head at something the gentleman was saying.

She watched Laura carefully. The attorney slowly rose to her feet, her eyes riveted upon Clara, as if her friend were strolling in Golden Gate Park with Rasputin.

"Ah, Mr. Farmer, I want you to meet my best friend and legal partner, Laura de Force Gordon. Laura, this is Aloysius Farmer. He lives just a few doors down from us. Our abodes share the same architectural design, it seems, although our décor has more of a transcontinental flavor."

The fat John Bunny doppelgänger smiled, his head nodding toward Laura. "I have agreed to purchase two of the paintings done by the owner, Miss Ah Toy. Have you purchased any of these fine works of art for your own pleasure, Miss Gordon?"

Trella noticed Laura's tight-lipped grin. "No, I am afraid my small apartment on Market Street behind my office barely has room for furniture and me. In fact, most of my clients are poor women who are really not interested in how much artwork I have accumulated on my walls. They simply want to stay out of prison."

She now understood that the rhetorical line was being drawn in the sand between her mother and Laura. Their competition would not cease until these two trials ended, one way or another.

"I completely understand. My clients are also women who are forced to take medicines simply because they cannot afford costlier yet perhaps much better surgical procedures. I just wish my daughter had come to me before taking matters into her own hands, when she became pregnant."

The crocodile tears rolled down his cheeks, and she imagined what a pig would look like if he were to cry. Dear Penny had accused him of being the father, of course, and this fact was quite unnerving.

He turned to address her. "Trella? I hope your thespian pursuits continue onto the stage. Mrs. Foltz tells me your brother, David, also has a love for acting. He is friends with Sarah Bernhardt. I tried to get Penny, my poor daughter, interested in the more cultured aspirations, as she did have a flair for the dramatic. Yet, as I explained to my new attorney, your mother, she was increasingly becoming ill with superstitions that only her mother, a Native Navajo, could have addressed."

"Thank you, Mr. Farmer. As my mother often remarks about her clients, you are now considered part of the family." She was thinking the opposite sentiment. Although she did realize the entire family would certainly be getting involved in his personal affairs as the trial played itself out.

"Good. Well, I am off to take care of business matters in the city. Thank goodness for our modern cable car network in San Francisco. They even have seats that can hold fellows of my wide girth."

She watched as he waddled to the door, took his derby off the coat rack, placed it on his head, and waited patiently until she opened the door for him. When the door was opened, he stepped out onto the porch and into the morning sunshine. Her mother stood behind her, and they both waved, as he awkwardly trundled his way down the steps and out toward California Street.

When she closed the door, she knew what was going to ensue, and she wouldn't have missed it for the world. Arguments between Laura and her mother were like watching a lioness confront an armadillo. Laura was constantly probing, stalking her prey in a crouch, testing, with her claws, the strength of the armadillo's ironclad and passive-aggressive shield of many-layered defenses, ready to bite into her mother the moment she found a frail one.

"Please. Do not start in, Laura. Let me tell you something before your invective begins to seethe from your mouth like lather." Laura circled her mother, and Clara kept moving to follow Laura's ever-widening arc inside the parlor. Trella said a prayer for Ah Toy's expensive standing sculptures from the Fifth Century in Southern China, one of which, a tall Goddess Mazu, Laura was now fingering as she strode along the carpet.

"The crux at the core of both of our cases is Penelope Farmer, is it not?" Laura probed.

She knew her mother's usual deductive logic would establish the argument, if that's what it was to be. Clara also knew Laura preferred to get to heart of a matter, so that's what she was giving her friend. For the moment, Clara remained silent.

"I plan to interview the entire staff of the Farmer mansion. Especially Mrs. Crutchfield, the girl's tutor. I need to know what she was reading, what her mental health was like, and of what her daily diet consisted." Laura nodded to herself, as if she were mentally checking off a list.

"Yes! In fact, I am going to be going even further in that direction. I will interview both Penelope and her mother, Haseya."

Both she and Laura stared fixedly at Clara.

"They are both dead. Are you joking?" Laura said.

Trella suddenly knew the answer. "Adeline," she blurted out.

Her mother nodded. "Yes. My future daughter-in-law, Adeline Quantrill, may be able to communicate with the past or present incarnation of one or both of these women. I plan to seek that information and possibly use it against the representatives of these private and public so-called 'philanthropic' organizations. We both know what they want, and it's not too different from what we discovered at the Stockton State Insane Asylum. These institutions often prey upon and profit from the public's sins and the unwanted children of those sins."

Laura shook her head until her curled black tresses whipped against her cheeks. "Perhaps I should have you committed back into the asylum. No court will ever accept testimony based upon the words of a spiritualist."

"Perhaps. And perhaps not. If I have a person who can vouch for its veracity, and then back it up with interviews of the participating parties, such as the staff, and your client, Mrs. Fulbright." Clara smiled.

"My client? She is being prosecuted for manslaughter!" Laura was turning red.

"That doesn't mean the judge will prevent her from testifying in my civil trial. She is innocent until proven guilty, remember? Also, there is one suffragette I have in mind, who presently resides in the English lap of luxury. Like you, she once made her money as a spiritualist, and she came under the personal patronage of one Mr. Cornelius Vanderbilt of New York, where she and her sister learned how to make *real* money. On Wall Street."

Laura gasped. "The Scarlet Sisters? Victoria and Tennessee Claflin?"

Clara nodded. She had never seen her mother so full of mirth. "Absolutely! Not only can they verify the efficacy of communicating with the afterlife, they can astound these men with the philosophy and politics of women and what they can do when they have rights. As a presidential candidate in 1872, Victoria can also give these male jurors some insight into national politics."

Laura was beginning to understand the possible consequences. "I see. Well then, as we are partners, Mrs. Foltz, then you would not have any problem lending me their expertise in my own case. I am thinking of teaching my jurors about their philosophy of Free Love."

Her mother laughed. "Of course, Laura! The international press will be haunting those court rooms like the ghosts of Penny and Haseya Farmer."

"Bow-wow-wow-yip-yip-yowee!"

Coming from just outside Toy mansion, perhaps even on the porch, the three women could hear the coyote's song. Trella knew the mystical symbolism of that call, and she realized it would be only a few days before she understood its actual importance.

Chapter 3: Deep Discovery

The Farmer Mansion, Twelve Nob Hill, San Francisco, June 24, 1887.

Clara had her discovery list of possible witnesses prepared. The initial three were employed by her client, Aloysius Farmer. With their new telephone installed, she was able to call ahead to inform them of her visit. Mrs. Althea Crutchfield told her she would be at the mansion at ten, so she was going to first ask questions of the two live-in staff members, the housekeeper, Madeline O'Rourke, and the chauffeur, Edward Barnes.

As this was a civil trial, the burden of proof for the plaintiff was not as stringent. They must prove with a "preponderance of evidence" rather than "beyond any reasonable doubt." It was the quality of said evidence that was of utmost importance and not the quantity. After reading the written accusations against her client, she was going to begin by pursuing two avenues of defense. The opposition was attempting to prove a "wrongful death," so she needed to gather discovery evidence to counter whatever proof the plaintiff had. As Laura Gordon pointed out, in a different, more just world, Farmer would be prosecuted for rape and manslaughter, but the real world was run by men. Therefore, Laura was defending the woman being accused in criminal court, the midwife, Mrs. Fulbright.

Because of the two hundred fifty thousand dollars being sought after in damages, the charge being made was one of negligence, even though Penelope's confession named Mr. Farmer as the parent of the deceased child. Therefore, the plaintiff would need to prove all three elements required in a negligence civil case, which are: duty of care, a breach of that duty, and proving that Mr. Farmer's actions directly caused the deaths of his daughter and her child in the womb.

Since they already had the deathbed statement of the victim, Penelope Farmer, naming her client as the father, one avenue she thought might be possible would be to prove that Penelope's declaration was nullified because of her mental state when she made it. In other words, she needed to explore whether or not the girl was mentally ill and was not aware of what she was doing, and, most especially, with whom she was doing it. The journal found in the park was also allegedly written by Penelope Farmer on the day of her death inside the Chinatown clinic. That was her first avenue of discovery. Dr. Andrew McFarland, with whom she had worked during the Stockton Insane Asylum and Supreme Court assassination cases, had agreed to work with her on this case, even though he could not examine the deceased girl. McFarland told her if she could get enough information about her behavior before the abortion from the father and others, then he could make some educated assumptions that she might use in court. Of course, there were also the psychic powers of Adeline, which she planned to use as a way to introduce the Navajo and Spiritualist links to this unique case.

Her second avenue was to use the testimony of Victoria and Tennessee Claflin to show the jury why organizations represented by the plaintiff want to profit from women who seek illegal abortions. These women are too poor to afford children, so the organizations are able to take these orphans in and then reap a bounty from selling the babies they give birth to on the open market to parents who cannot have children.

In addition, they use these children as cheap labor, especially when they are immigrants, coloreds, or the destitute whites. In order to tantalize the press and the jury with the spirit world, she would use Adeline to channel Penelope Farmer and her mother. The Claflin sisters could then testify about how Spiritualism serves as a sounding board for women's rights in a world where men rule every other conventional religious pulpit.

This tactic would refute the plaintiff's attempt to show Mr. Farmer as the cause of the death of his daughter. Instead, she would demonstrate how he had been following the law all along and that it was the society, which forces women to seek abortions because they are pressured by conventional religious beliefs, and the profit motive of the ones who seek to benefit from live births of unwanted children. To accomplish this plan, she would use the Claflin sisters to help her investigate the plaintiff's representative organization, Edgewood, the San Francisco Protestant Asylum, the oldest such entity. This was the group that filed the lawsuit in the first place. She learned from Captain Isaiah Lees, her lover, that one stood the best chance at finding scandal by interviewing those who knew where the money was taken in and how it was handled.

She already knew that these private and public orphanages were tax-exempt, even though the State had no direct supervisorial role over their daily activities. The State of California, because of its history of a nomadic and mostly male population, developed a very *laissez-faire* attitude toward the welfare of miscreants and the poor. In effect, these orphanages were very similar to the State Insane Asylums and other public hospitals, and she had a great deal of experience with those entities, especially with the Stockton State Insane Asylum.

She also knew that in addition to the money they were getting from private, religious subscriptions and donations from the wealthy of San Francisco, many of them were directly subsidized by the State. These organizations were able to make money from their orphans by placing them into indentured servitude until the age of 21, for males, and 18, for females. That made for quite a lot of money coming into these private and incorporated "welfare" organizations. They collected the children's wages, a state subsidy, and a tax-free income, in return for the child's limited education, food, clothing and shelter.

The front entrance had big Greek columns and a wide portico, with brick steps leading up to the door. They had a garden out front with bronze fencing on three sides. As she walked up the forty-five steps leading to the porch, she was thinking about the questions she would ask. She already knew the basics about the three people, as Mr. Farmer had given her the details during his recent visit. Her main purpose was to find out if they had any inside information about the mother and daughter who had lived here.

Mrs. O'Rourke answered the door, and Mr. Barnes was already waiting in the kitchen. Madeline O'Rourke had worked for

Farmer for the past six years, and she was older, sixty-two, with a heavy-set frame and a height of five-two. Her white-laced blouse was open at the collar, and a large crucifix dangled between her ample bosoms. Her black skirt was bell-shaped from wide, child-bearing hips, and her maid's cap was also black.

After she sat down, and opened her notepad, she discovered from the chauffer, who had worked for Mr. Farmer for twelve years, that the mansion was constructed by the same architect, Augustus Laver. Laver also designed Ah Toy's home and the James Clair Flood mansion near the top of Nob Hill. All three homes were replica two-story Brownstones meant to emulate the East Coast mansions of the wealthy. Whereas most of the mansions on Nob Hill, including the Hopkins mansion, were made of wood, these three homes were made of stone masonry.

"Mr. Farmer likes to take the cable car down California to his office on Market, but I take him to his social functions in other parts of the city."

Mr. Barnes was a thin, fifty-eight-year-old Negro, about five feet, eight inches tall, and he wore the usual black gabardines, brass buttons shaped in a triangular pattern on the front of his jacket, with matching cap and visor. He had a thin mustache and a personable smile.

"As you both are probably aware, I am representing your employer in a civil lawsuit brought against him by a collection of San Francisco orphan homes and charities. I need to know more information about the ladies of the house. I know that Penelope's mother, Haseya, was a Navajo tribal member. She died three years ago from consumption. Were either of you here when she was ill?"

They both nodded, but Madeline looked down at her freckled hands and sighed.

"Mrs. O'Rourke? Did you observe anything out of the ordinary between any of the family members?"

She was expecting the usual tale of emotional temper tantrums and perhaps personal attacks. She was hoping there weren't visits to Penelope's room by Mr. Farmer.

"The most ungodly mischief I ever seen! I go to bed at ten,

and these walls are thick. Never heard a peep before that night. But when the mother came down with consumption, after they got back from their Arizona visit to her tribe, I began to hear a strange barking at night. Then, over the next few nights, I could hear someone thrashing around inside the mother's room next-door. On the third night, I opened my bedroom door a crack, to look out, you know?"

She made the sign of the cross.

"And I seen the little lass race down the hall toward me. Like her black hair was on fire. She was crouched over, her head raised up. She stopped in her tracks. And then she howled. Never seen or heard the likes of it before. When I told her about it the next day, she just smiled at me, but she never spoke another word from that day forward. Her mother died three days later."

Mr. Barnes nodded. "She's right about the girl not talking. Even Mrs. Crutchfield complained about the girl being mum. I live in the colored section of the city, so I don't know about what happens here at night. The girl was most always in the library, during the day. I do know that. I did take them all shopping after they returned from Arizona."

"Did you see any signs the girl was pregnant? Was anything ever mentioned?" She wanted to probe the areas in which the plaintiff might be interested.

"No. I'm not married, so I wouldn't know what to look for," Barnes said.

Mrs. O'Rourke raised her hand, as if she were in school. "Me and my three girls all had children, and we all got the morning sickness. Penelope had it too. I seen her heave up her toes many times. She even vomited on the day she left to see Mrs. Fulbright."

That was interesting. Did O'Rourke know about the abortionist?

"How did you know she was going to see Mrs. Fulbright?"

The maid smiled. "Oh, I never knew about it then. I read about it in the paper. I put two and two together afterwards. When she died. At the time, I thought little Penny was ill because of her mother's death. If I known she was going to get her baby murdered . . ." she again made the sign of the cross. "That Fulbright woman should be hanged! It's a mortal sin what she does. Jesus preserve us all!"

That brought up an interesting dilemma she wanted to now investigate.

"Does either of you know how Mr. Farmer makes his income?"

They both began to fidget in their chairs.

"Well?" Her voice was adamant.

"Mr. Farmer told us both about his business when we first began to work here. Because of the demonstrators who came to visit almost every month," Barnes said.

"And Mr. Farmer ain't no abortionist! He's a Protestant, but he's no abortionist. He showed us the label that goes on each bottle of Dr. Goody's Female medicine he sells. It says, in all capital letters NOT FOR PREGNANT WOMEN," Mrs. O'Rourke explained, nodding her head for emphasis.

"It's a medication to help women have better menstrual flows, is how he explained it," Barnes said. "He told us these demonstrators were riled up by what that U. S. Postal Inspector said."

"Anthony Comstock?" She knew this gentleman very well. He was certain to be one of the plaintiff's main witnesses.

"That's him. Mr. Farmer says that Comstockery is making women get all kinds of female diseases that can be prevented by what my boss sells. People demonstrate when some ignorant woman takes Dr. Goody's potions after they get pregnant. Boss calls it 'drinking the pennyroyal tea.' That's akin to suicide."

She was getting all her client's products analyzed by a chemist. They were certain to become a major focus during the trial. Pennyroyal, she knew, was a main ingredient in the female menstrual potion Farmer sold, and Clara knew it would be a major bone of contention. In her cursory research, she knew that for hundreds of years, before surgery was available to women, they used pennyroyal to prevent pregnancy. It was an unassuming flower, with its small, pointed, lavender petals cupped by deep green leaves. Pennyroyal flowers grew in tiny clusters that thread a single, delicate stem. In small doses, it helps to improve menstrual flow. She also knew that at higher doses it can also kill.

"Mrs. Foltz?" A tall woman wearing spectacles and a dark gray dress with medium bustle entered the kitchen. She stood at the head of the table, at attention, surveying everyone with an overbearing manner. Her brown hair, rolled into a bun, was streaked with gray, and she had the studious, pursed lips of a teacher.

"Yes, Mrs. Crutchfield. I am so happy you could come. Won't you be seated?"

Clara knew the woman was fifty-two, a mother of three, who had served as a private tutor for fifteen years. Before that she was a principal at a girls' academy in San Jose for ten years. Aloysius Farmer said he hired her because she was an expert at teaching young girls the True Woman Method. Mr. Farmer and Trella Evelyn informed her that this curriculum gave daughters of the wealthy elite the basic skills they needed to run a household. The practical skills of mathematics, reading, and writing. She must also, at all times, be subservient to the male head of the household and to the same patriarchy that controlled all of society.

The tutor used a handkerchief to wipe off the seat of the kitchen chair before she sat down. She frowned at Mr. Barnes and Mrs. O'Rourke.

"Do you mind? I have some private information to share with Mrs. Foltz."

Clara stood up to shake hands with the two regular employees.

"Thank you for your assistance," she said.

All the other staff were day workers who left the mansion after their chores were completed. What she needed to know about Penelope Farmer could possibly be given to her by the tutor now sitting across from her.

"As you know, Mrs. Crutchfield, I am defending Mr. Farmer. I have been a teacher in my early years, so I am very sympathetic to your duties. I need to know the truth about what his daughter was doing, as you can be a very important resource for my defense." She smiled at the teacher. "What is this personal information you have for me?"

The tutor nodded slowly. "I understand. I must be frank with you, Mrs. Foltz. I am not a person who necessarily believes what she teaches. Were you a public school teacher?"

"Yes. In Iowa and Indiana." She was interested in this line of thought. It might mean Crutchfield had a better insight into the girl's character than she had initially expected.

"As you must know, teaching in the public environment requires an adherence to established policies. When I became principal in San Jose, I suddenly had to learn the private sector's practices. In the private sector, for the most part, you do what the parents require."

"I am quite familiar with the differences. My daughter attends a public university, and I have had personal dealings with Mr. Leland Stanford and his policies at that private university." She did not want to discuss the problems she had with Stanford's support of Eugenics and her recent experiences at the Stockton State Insane Asylum.

"I am an avowed suffragist. What I teach to these wealthy elites is simply pecuniary in nature. I can make more money. What I have to tell you about Penelope and her family is because I am a supporter of women's rights." She took out a sheet of paper from her gray handbag, unfolded it on the table, and ran a forefinger down a list she had compiled.

"Thank you for the honesty. Although I am defending your employer, I still want to know the truth. If there have been illegal activities going on, then I am bound by legal ethics to report them to the proper authorities."

She was hoping she could continue in her defense of Mr. Farmer, as she also needed the money.

"It all began when the family returned from Arizona. The mother, as you know, was Navajo. Despite what Mr. Farmer instructed me to do, I could not get Penelope to learn anything unless I agreed to listen to the two females' demands concerning what the tribe believes. Mrs. Farmer, who spoke no English, was translated by the girl, and I have made a list of their four most important beliefs, so you can see for yourself why I am now concerned."

"Please. Illuminate me."

She lifted her pencil, ready to write it down on the pad.

"First of all, the Navajo people, the Diné, pass through three different worlds before emerging into this world, the Fourth World, or Glittering World. The Diné believe there are two classes of beings: the Earth People and the Holy People. The Holy People are believed to have the power to aid or harm the Earth People. Since Earth People of the Diné are an integral part of the universe, they must do everything they can to maintain harmony or balance on Mother Earth."

"I can see how your True Woman curricula would differ with these beliefs. There is no mention of male or female in this Navajo legend."

She was very intrigued. She might use this information as a possible reason why Penelope would become mentally confused or not know the consequence of her own actions.

"Yes. Secondly, the four directions are represented by four colors: White Shell represents the east, Turquoise the south, Yellow Abalone the west, and Jet Black the north. In the Navajo culture there are four directions, four seasons, the first four clans and four colors that are associated with the four sacred mountains. In most Navajo rituals there are four songs and multiples thereof, as well as Navajo wedding basket and many other symbolic uses of four."

"And you have four items on your list. I assume we are now reaching the important practices," she guessed.

"Indeed, we are. When the mother, Haseya, was diagnosed with fatal consumption, she called in the Medicine Man from her tribe. Because I was charged with Penelope's education, I was allowed to listen to what the holy man told her. He said the disease she had was because of a curse placed on the family from a Holy person visiting from one of the three other worlds."

"What did they do to cause this curse?" She wrote down the facts and leaned forward in expectation.

"He told them Mr. Farmer was an Earth Person who was going against the harmony of Mother Earth in the Glittering World.

He told Haseya and Dezba, which is the girl's tribal name, that they had to use their powers as *yee naaldooshii* to put Aloysius back on a harmonious path."

"What do those words mean? What were their powers?" She wanted a term she could better describe to a jury.

"Dezba means war. *Yee naaldooshii* means skinwalkers, as the mother later explained to me. Skinwalkers are Holy People who can change into an animal to protect the sacred ancestral traditions."

"Very interesting. Women who protect the tribal law. Is there anything else?" She wrote down the term "skinwalker" and circled it.

"Yes. They were told they must lose their lives, if need be, to protect the harmony. However, in retribution, four evil Earth people in the Glittering World would eventually lose their lives."

"In retribution? You mean, after Haseya and Dezba died?" This was special information to perhaps be explored by psychic Adeline Quantrill.

"Yes. Two evil Earth people must die for each Holy skinwalker who dies. You see, according to the Medicine Man, the animal possession abilities of skinwalker witches do not die with their bodies. They continue in the Glittering World as spirit advocates for the Diné."

"Advocates? Sounds almost like a lawyer. Or ghosts. Do you mean these spirit entities will kill people?" She wanted some place to hang her rhetorical hat.

"Yes. Kill. Now I am going to tell you the most frightening experience that I've ever had in my life—both in and out of a classroom filled with maniacal students. It happened after Mrs. Farmer passed away from the curse, or from the consumption, whichever culture is your preference."

It was Mrs. Crutchfield's turn to lean forward. The lenses in her spectacles reflected the light beaming down from the new electric bulb installed inside the small overhead chandelier. It was as if some kind of spiritual presence had entered her brain from another world.

Clara shivered involuntarily. "Go on. I'm listening," she

said.

The entire kitchen seemed to get warmer. The stove was not on. The electric light could not emit that much heat. She believed a spiritual presence had entered them both, as a warning.

"After the funeral, Penny began to take over all the household duties. She became officious, organized and efficient, just like her mother. However, she also did all of this the way her mother had done it. Without speaking."

"She never spoke to anybody?" She wrote it down. It validated what Mrs. O'Rourke had told her.

"She did not speak. I obviously could not teach her any lessons. She became obsessed. And then, the week she left the house to go to the midwife in Chinatown, she began to wear her mother's clothing. And, then came the most provoking change. I saw her face and mannerisms transform into the exact duplicate of Haseya Farmer."

"Are you certain? Were you tired or under any pressure at the time?" She wanted a sworn statement, as she predicted her opponent's questioning the woman's mental state.

"I was leaving the house, and she turned toward me after coming out of the master bedroom. When I addressed her, she spoke to me for the first time in weeks. She said exactly what her mother always said, *Hágoónee*. The Navajo never says goodbye. She says 'all right then.' I had no answer, of course. I was too dumbfounded to reply."

"Are you willing to testify to this under oath, Mrs. Crutchfield? I will need the exact date and time as well."

She could take the risk to convince a jury. This testimony would combine well with her other excursions into the unknown. Her father, also a lawyer, always told her that taking chances with stories was far more effective with a jury than tedious expert testimony.

"It was June 20. I remember the time. I gazed at the grandfather clock that stood in the bedroom hall next to her mother's room. The time was 4:04 PM. The fours startled me."

Clara could feel the perspiration run down her back, between her breasts, and over her face. It was like an oven.

The distinct yipping and yapping howl of the coyote caused them to stand up from their chairs at the kitchen table. Their eyes were wide in expectant fear, as they listened to the continuing cry of the animal. It was coming from outside, but its penetrating song made the room hotter, if that were indeed possible.

"And ... that was what I heard from her on the day she became the image of her mother. Her face, in the shadows of early twilight, momentarily transformed into the quivering snout, the flashing teeth, and the howling snarl of a coyote."

Clara moved over to where Mrs. Crutchfield was standing. She took the older woman's hands into her own. She could feel the sweat, and she could feel the tremoring shivers from both of their appendages.

"I must confess to you as well," she whispered.

"What do you mean, confess?" the teacher stared, mesmerized by Clara's hazel eyes.

"I heard the same howl this morning, after Mr. Farmer left my home. How do you suppose these skinwalkers move so fast? Also, how do they kill humans?" She was captured by her own fear, so her questions were coming from the illogical, hot-white core of that same trepidation.

"They run on all fours, and they can run two-hundred miles in one evening. The Medicine Man said that if you accidentally lock eyes with a skinwalker, it can absorb itself into your body and take control of your actions."

Clara tried to make her voice louder, but it came out of her mouth as a squealing sound. "How do they kill?"

"He told us they enchant the powder of corpses and use the substance as a poison dust on victims."

When the lights went out, they both screamed.

Chapter 4: Quickening

Ingleside Jail, Ocean House Road, San Francisco, June 24, 1887.

Laura and Ah Toy had visited the Ingleside Jail during last year's case involving the murder of wealthy San Francisco husbands by their wives. Her client, Rachel Rafferty, was the wife accused of manslaughter in the death of her husband. She was never able to defend her because Rafferty was poisoned in her cell. Laura was convinced there were people who wanted Mrs. Honora Fulbright dead also, and she was pleased to see Fulbright had been placed inside the maximum-security building when they arrived at the Superintendent's Office on the second floor of the main building.

Ah Toy, at age fifty-nine, was a beautiful woman. She wore a long red and gold silk dress called a *cheongsam* that extended down to cover her once-bound feet, and her hair was still mostly black, although waves of gray were present in her short style, and her bangs were completely white.

She wanted Ah Toy to be with her because she now knew that her client, although her married name was Fulbright, was Chinese, and her maiden name was Woo Changying. Although she spoke perfect English, as she was a graduate of Berkeley, the cultural references she might make could best be explained by Ah Toy. The elder woman was a family friend of Clara's for many years, harkening back to Ah Toy's days as a successfully independent bordello madam in Chinatown. Clara had legally represented her on many occasions, and they had become best of friends over the years.

Superintendent Hector Gonzales was there to greet them and explain the special arrangements for her client. He was a dandy in his brown herringbone tweed sack coat and black derby. She could see a gold watch chain dangling from his inside vest. All the trendiest men had begun wearing the shorter sack coat, which had replaced the traditional frock. His thick black hair and handlebar mustache matched the black leather couch and matching chair for his giant African blackwood desk. The flags of the United States and California stood on either side of the desk, and the photo of Governor and former San Francisco Mayor, Washington Bartlett, hung on the wall behind. Above the governor's photo was a one-by-two-foot crucifix.

His hands reached out to her, and she took them, although she would have preferred to shake right hands as equals. His black eyes penetrated hers with that inner confidence that men have when they make it up the political ladder of bureaucracy.

"Attorney Gordon! *Buenas dias*! I am finally able to meet you."

"Thank you, Superintendent. Have there been any irregularities with my client? You have her under maximum security, and I appreciate that."

She watched his full black eyebrows furrow.

"I trust you have read the newspapers. As you came in, did you happen to see all the demonstrators?"

"Yes, but I was referencing her safety *inside* the prison. Last year, as you recall, my client Mrs. Rafferty was poisoned by a person who infiltrated your security."

She assumed he was more concerned about the negative publicity than he was about protecting Mrs. Fulbright.

Before speaking, Superintendent Gonzales took a Cuban cigar from a black humidor on his desk. They were pre-cut, so he stuck it between his lips, raised the lighter up to the tip, struck the wheel with his thumb, and the flame ignited the rolled tobacco at once. As he began to puff, she watched the smoke curl over his head. He was dark-complexioned, and he never once acknowledged the presence of Ah Toy. Her client was also Chinese. Was there perhaps a connection?

"I want my associate, Miss Ah Toy, to accompany me. My client is also Chinese. Do you have a problem with that?"

She watched his face. That same political smile spread across his swarthy demeanor.

"Why not? Most of the counter-demonstrators have been Chinese. *Cuantos más, mejor.*"

He marched over to a long cabinet filled with keys.

The more the merrier, indeed, she thought. She took Spanish in college, and she detested linguistic subterfuge.

"Here you are, attorney. Cellblock H, Cell 16. There are two armed guards at the cell, and Sergeant-at-Arms Robles will escort you."

He pushed a red button on his desk. His door opened, and a short man with a flowing black mustache, who wore a blue guard's uniform with sergeant's stripes and matching cap, filled the doorway. His girth was even wider than Clara's client, Aloysius Farmer. The superintendent carried the key over to his sergeant and placed it in the palm of his hand, as if he were bestowing the key to the city and not to a jail cell.

"*Por favor*, follow me," Sergeant Robles said, and she watched him waddle out into the hallway.

She could barely see around the posterior of Sergeant Robles, but when he finally unlocked the cell door and opened it, she could finally gaze at her client, Mrs. Fulbright. She was wearing steel shackles around her ankles and her wrists; she was slumped over, seated on the narrow metal cot. Her gray jail smock was soiled, and it was stifling inside the cell, like an oven. There were flies buzzing in the air and landing everywhere, especially inside the odoriferous chamber pot in the corner. She saw a rat the size of a cat scurry from one hole in the baseboard of the cell into another. She tried to contain her anger, but it was very difficult.

"Sergeant Robles. Do you suppose they have shackles that can fit you?" She wanted to get his attention, and she thought the escalation of her sarcasm might do the trick.

"*Que*? It is for her protection. Superintendent Gonzales has ordered it." He wiped his sweaty forehead with the back of his forearm, staring down at Mrs. Fulbright, who was now peering up at these visitors to her domain.

Her eyelids were drooping. Mucus was running from her nose, and her spectacles were fogged and smudged. Her black hair was cut shorter than normal, and her posture was poor. Otherwise, she was a very attractive young woman of thirty-eight.

Laura walked over to the edge of the cot, stooped over, and stared into her client's dark eyes.

"Mrs. Fulbright? Can you hear me?"

"Yes. Attorney Gordon? I have been waiting for you. My husband, I am afraid, has not been allowed to see me as yet. I was hoping you could . . ." Her voice trailed off.

Ah Toy spoke to her client in Cantonese.

She replied.

Ah Toy turned to her, "She says a Chinese Inspector from the U. S. Customs Collectors came yesterday. He has levied a fine on her for working at criminal activities here. They are, as a result, preparing deportation papers under a special writ of the Alien Contract Labor Laws of 1885 and this year."

"When she married Albert Fulbright, a very wealthy merchant here in San Francisco, she became a United States citizen. Also, she was born in Chinatown, in the United States, so she is not an immigrant. Finally, she should not be fined for performing so-called criminal activities unless she were convicted of such activities. I shall be in touch with Customs when we finish here. Please tell her this."

Ah Toy spoke again, this time in both English and Cantonese. Mrs. Fulbright's wan smile was her response.

"Now. Sergeant-at-Arms Robles. Unless you wish to have your arms manacled in the same manner as my client, I suggest you take her encumbrances away. Also, get one of those guards—or both of them—to clean this cell up. Or, I shall get the California Health Department to issue a warrant for the arrest of you and your superintendent."

He fidgeted with the pistol in the holster around his wide waist and frowned.

"You are in violation of health codes and Section Five, Article One of the Declaration of Rights in the California Constitution. It states, and I quote, 'Excessive bail shall not be required, nor excessive fines imposed, nor shall cruel and unusual punishments be inflicted, nor shall witnesses be unreasonably detained.' If you wish to pursue it further, you can always appeal to

41

the Supreme Court. However, they have the same amendment in their number eight. Sad, but true. *Buenos dias, señor!*"

She expected the poor sergeant understood little of what she told him, but his actions belied his ignorance. Both guards entered the cell, without their rifles, unlocked Mrs. Fulbright from her confines, and began to hastily take the blanket, pillowcase and sheet off the cot. They also quickly returned with two chairs for her and Ah Toy to sit on.

"Please, come back later to sweep, mop, and trap the rodents, if you would." She smiled.

The sergeant left with his charges. She at last could speak in private with her client. Next time, she would insist they have a clean, quiet room, with some type of air conditioning. Perhaps even Superintendent Gonzales's office.

"Do you prefer to converse in Cantonese or in English? Or, perhaps both?" She took the woman's hands in her own. She was trying to be more like Clara in her approach to clients.

Mrs. Fulbright looked over at Ah Toy. She said something in Cantonese.

"She prefers to use both," Ah Toy said.

"Very well. As your attorney, I am here to defend you from the charge of manslaughter made against you by the State. I will be representing you in the court room, if we go that far, but I first need to assure you that everything you tell me will be held in strictest confidence. Is that clear?" She looked over at Ah Toy, but the woman smiled and nodded. She was, after all, a Berkeley graduate.

"Also, you have an obligation to tell me the truth. If I learn or discover that something you tell me is without foundation, I shall immediately resign as your defense attorney."

Again, the woman nodded.

"I shall also be interviewing others in order to verify and expound upon what you tell me, and I may later ask you for clarification concerning evidence that may arise. My first questions will concern what happened between you and Miss Penelope Farmer. Most especially, what happened on the day of Monday, June 20th. Is that understood?"

"Of course," her client replied, but Laura was hoping she was not intellectually challenged because of the mistreatment.

"When did you first speak with Miss Farmer?"

Mrs. Fulbright rubbed her arms where the shackles had been, and they were still red at the wrists, where the metal gripped her thin forearms.

"I only spoke with her once. Over the telephone. She responded to an advertisement I had in the Classified section of the *Chronicle*. Many women do the same thing."

"Do you remember what your advertisement says?" She knew the prosecution would know this, so she wanted to verify. "Ah Toy, could you copy this statement? Also, please check the newspaper to verify."

Ah Toy nodded and took out a small notepad and pencil from her gold handbag with a red dragon on the side.

"My services are advertised to conform with the Comstock laws and the Obstetrics Society. I never speak negatively concerning pregnancy or the birth of a child. I simply tell interested married women that I will assist in the delivery of the child they carry, and if they have any problems, I can refer them to a proper obstetrician. I cannot mention abortion, of course, in my advertisements. I am a midwife with over twenty years' experience. I use the accepted words in the ad such as suppression, irregularity, obstruction, etcetera. I can remove their problem in a very short time."

"That's noteworthy. Did you copy that, Ah Toy?" Her friend nodded. "Do women who read your ads understand that you also help them when they're unmarried?"

"Yes. Despite what the present medical establishment believes, women still communicate about abortion in a private manner. Sadly, the only time an abortion gets recorded and is defamed is when a mother dies. Nobody knows about the thousands of successful procedures that are accomplished with no ill side effects."

"I understand. This is the present problem. I must defend you in a criminal court, even though the law has accepted the deathbed accusation of the minor mother about her father being the impregnator. Under law, the fetus has no legal rights. In 1884, speaking about the case of *Dietrich v. Inhabitants of Northampton*, Judge Oliver Wendell Holmes stated the rule concerning the rights of a fetus. He said that any injury suffered in the womb, from the outside, which causes the child to die, cannot be a cause of legal action. Why? Because the child, until it is born, is legally a part of the mother and does not have legal personhood."

Mrs. Fulbright looked confused. "I don't understand. If the court has stated that the child is not a legal person until live birth, then how can any action taken by me be considered the cause of the mother's death? The examining physician told me Miss Farmer died of bleeding caused by an ectopic pregnancy. The fetus was growing inside the fallopian tube, which had been misshapen due to a genetic growth inside."

It was Laura's turn to be confused. She knew about the report by the coroner, which stated that the death of the mother was caused by an ectopic miscarriage, but this information about the private physician was completely new.

"Who was this doctor? Did you call him when Penelope began to bleed? Will he testify on your behalf?"

"I don't believe he will. He works only in Chinatown. I don't think the court will recognize his expertise." Mrs. Fulbright bowed her head. "He is my superior, and he is also Chinese."

Ah Toy looked up from her transcribing. "I know him. When I was a Madame, he helped some of my ladies who got into trouble. Dr. Liu Wei. However, isn't he an acupuncturist?"

"Yes. And so am I," Mrs. Fulbright said.

"You are *what*? An acupuncturist?" Laura was astounded. "Isn't that placing pressure on different parts of the body—usually with needles?"

Her client looked up. "Yes. I am. Acupuncture is thousands of years old. It is a very revered medical practice."

She squeezed Mrs. Fulbright's hands. "Do you mean you did *not* use abortion instruments on Penny Farmer?"

"That's correct. I induce abortions by putting pressure on the untouchable points." Mrs. Fulbright looked over at Ah Toy and began talking to her in Cantonese.

After several minutes, Ah Toy, who had written down notes, explained what the woman had said.

"She never uses needles on the untouchable points. She uses pressure from her hands. There are six major acupressure points on the body that are believed to induce labor. She used three before the young woman began to go into labor. In Chinese, they are called *Sanyinjiao*, *Zhiyin*, and *Hegu*. Each of these is located at different places on the female anatomy."

"You mean to tell me that there was no surgical instrument inserted into that girl's womb?" Laura was aghast at the importance of what she was saying.

"Correct. She says when the girl began to scream and bleed, she stopped her pressure massages immediately. She called Dr. Wei, and when he came over, the girl had expired."

"You understand what this means, Ah Toy? It means that in order to prove that Mrs. Fulbright was the cause of Penelope Farmer's death, they will have to agree that acupuncture can induce labor." She smiled.

"Yes. And so?" Ah Toy was perplexed.

"Dr. Horatio Storer is the State's expert witness. He will never agree that Chinese medicine can ever accomplish anything modern Western surgery can do. We have the prosecution over a very large barrel. If he agrees that the Chinese can perform acupuncture-induced labor, then why would women want to go to one of his modern hospitals?"

Ah Toy cleared her throat.

"From the articles I have read, this doctor wants to shut down all midwives and doctors who perform abortions. What better way to demonstrate to the public that midwives—even ones who practice Chinese medicine—are responsible for so many deaths? Helping the prosecution prove that acupuncture can induce labor would be a good thing, would it not? It would put Mrs. Fulbright out of business."

Laura had to admit that Ah Toy was making an excellent argument. In fact, nothing was preventing the hospitals from hiring acupuncturists to help law-abiding pregnant women.

"You are, once again, showing your astute awareness and critical thinking skills. My lawyer's mind was reaching too far afield. We need to focus upon what the prosecution must prove. We need to demonstrate that Penelope's miscarriage would have occurred, even without the acupuncture pressure by Mrs. Fulbright."

"She never visited a doctor before coming to me. How can you show that her ectopic pregnancy was known before the miscarriage in my house?"

She liked the way Mrs. Fulbright was thinking. It would be a pleasure working with her.

"I have yet to interview the staff at her home. I can also question Mr. Farmer. He might have noticed something about his daughter, not knowing what it was. Do you know the symptoms that can be observed, Mrs. Fulbright?" She nodded at Ah Toy to take notes.

"The girl might have experienced sharp or stabbing pain that comes and goes and varies in intensity. She may also have had gastrointestinal symptoms."

"Such as?" She wanted everything to be as specific as possible, in case they needed to describe it in non-medical terms.

"Flatulence, diarrhoea, and vomiting. Also, weakness, dizziness, and fainting. And, of course, bleeding."

"Superb. Ah Toy, we shall need those terms for when we question our prospective witnesses. Can you show me where these points are? On my body?" She moved her chair over to sit next to Mrs. Fulbright on the cot.

"Very well. Give me your left arm."

She extended her arm, and her client took it gingerly between her hands. She moved her right hand to the web skin between her thumb and forefinger. She placed her thumb at a point just to the left of the knuckle on her forefinger and began to gently massage it, with her right thumb on the spot and her forefinger beneath.

"This is *Hegu*, the joining valley. On an acupuncture map or dummy of the body, it is the large intestine, or LI4. Applying pressure can induce labor, relieve pain, and strengthen immunity." Her client stopped massaging.

"I can't say that I feel differently. Sorry," she said.

Mrs. Fulbright pointed at her left foot. "Please, take off your shoe."

She reached down and unlaced her black boot. She pulled it off and allowed it to fall to the floor of the cell, displaying her long black stocking.

"Take the stocking off as well. I need to grasp your foot in my hands."

She pulled off the long stocking, reached over to get the boot, and tucked the stocking inside. She let the boot again fall. Her client bent over, grasped her left foot, and raised it into her lap.

"This is *Zhiyin*, or reaching yin. The bladder 67 point, BL67, is located on the outside of the end of the pinky toe, near the edge of the nail." She placed her right hand at that location, and she began to pinch the toe, with her thumb and index finger.

"Now that seems to feel quite nice. What does it do?" She wiggled her other toes and smiled.

"The *Zhiyin* point is believed to turn the fetus and stimulate uterine contractions."

"I see. And since the fetus was not inside the uterus of Penelope, would it still cause the turning and contractions?" She wanted something to talk about on the witness stand.

"I don't know. Possibly." Mrs. Fulbright stopped the pinching and sat up. She pointed at her right boot. "Please, take off the other boot."

She repeated the unlacing, pulled off her sock, inserted it inside, and dropped the boot. She lifted her right foot onto the cot.

"The spleen 6 point, SP6, is one of the more versatile and commonly used points. It's used for many conditions, including labor induction. *Sanyinjiao*--or three yin intersection--SP6 is located above the ankle, on the backside of the shinbone. It's about the distance of four finger widths above the inner ankle bone."

Her client reached over to grab her calf. "Use the index finger to apply firm pressure on the point for a few seconds. Take a minute break before repeating."

"I can really feel that. It is quite luxurious. May I put my shoes back on now?"

"Yes, you may. Those are the three points I used on the girl. I did not have time to pressure the other three."

As she was putting her second shoe on, Sergeant-at-Arms Robles returned. He was escorting two men. One man she knew at once. He was Captain of Detectives of the San Francisco Police Department, Isaiah W. Lees, who also happened to be her legal partner Clara's lover. Lees wore his usual civilian uniform, a brown frock coat and vest with checkered pants and spit-shined Oxfords. He immediately turned his contemplative scowl into a smile when he saw her and Ah Toy through the bars.

The other gentleman was a head shorter than the tall detective. He wore a dark-gray suit with a bowed necktie, and a matching vest and watch fob. His hair was receding far back on his forehead, and his full beard was graying and neatly trimmed. He stood back from the cell door and stared inside, as if he were a patron at the zoo.

Sergeant Robles unlocked the cell door. "Mrs. Gordon? Superintendent Gonzales says your time is up for today. You may come back tomorrow. Dr. Storer has made reservations to speak with Mrs. Fulbright."

So, it was Horatio Robinson Storer. The man who had almost single-handedly made abortion a criminal act. She got up from the cot and stood next to her client. She crossed her arms across her chest.

"Isaiah. You know better than to ask questions of my client without my being in the room." She raised her eyebrows and pursed her plain, full lips.

Both men followed the portly jailer's wave into the cell.

"Laura, it's so good to hear your kind greetings once more. I shall not be asking *any* questions of your client. I am merely here to allow Dr. Storer to meet Mrs. Fulbright as a fellow obstetric

48

professional. Nothing about her case is going to be discussed. You have my word."

She turned back toward the small woman, her client, who was still seated on the narrow cot. She was cleaning her spectacles on her jail smock.

"If they ask you any questions concerning your case, do not reply. You may only respond to questions about your profession, as that is still part of discovery. Nothing about what you did on the day you met with Penelope Farmer. Is that clear?"

Mrs. Fulbright nodded.

Dr. Storer approached her and extended his hand. His face was beaming. She shook it and felt the perspiration. He was obviously nervous to be within such surroundings.

"Attorney Gordon. I am honored. I merely wish to enquire as to your client's health and well-being. My profession is one of constant study and improvement. We shall make our medical advancements only through the vigilance of maintaining an open mind. You might even say this is a chance to intertwine the best obstetric practices of East and West."

She let her hand gently fall to her side, where she discreetly wiped it against her plain, navy dress, with no bustle.

"I understand, doctor. Were you aware that you and my client have quite different beliefs concerning the miracle of quickening? That moment when the pregnant woman can first feel the movement of her child?"

She smiled at him and motioned with her right hand to Ah Toy that they would soon be leaving. This was to be her parting salvo for this gentleman doctor from Harvard. She had recently read about how he had committed his first wife, Emily Elvira, to an insane asylum because she had refused to bear him more progeny. She was also the victim of frequent menstrual disorders, which, to her, added to the irony of his putting his wife away.

"If we have proved the existence of fetal life before quickening has taken place, or can take place, and by all analogy and a close and conclusive process of scientific induction, its commencement at the very beginning, at conception itself, we are compelled to believe abortion is always a crime."

He seemed to have his words memorized from his many speeches on the topic over the last twenty years. She had been meditating on this subject ever since the girl was found dead.

"Quickening is not fast and scientific, however. We women have felt this miracle of a child's earliest movement inside us for thousands of years, well before men like you first decided you knew exactly *when* life began and even why life *should* begin. Women, such as Mrs. Fulbright, Ah Toy, myself, and millions of others around the world, wish to keep this decision about bringing a child into the world, private. We need to make this decision privately so that this important choice is made in our own and our family's best interest. Not *your* best interest. In *our* best interest, which must include physical, mental, economic, and even spiritual security considerations. Without the power to choose what we can do with our bodies, we are not women. We are not even human. We are mindless receptacles for your personal pleasures and your personal whims. The future, for us, does not exist. Good day to you, Dr. Storer. I hope to see you in court."

Chapter 5: Legal Gametes

The Toy Mansion, Fifteen Nob Hill, San Francisco, June 25, 1887.

I was appointed to take these notes at the kitchen table by attorney Clara Foltz, my mother. She and her legal partner, Laura Gordon, had begun a discussion of their upcoming trials during a brief rehearsal of my new play in the parlor. The actors in this play are my siblings and one dear friend, Ah Toy. However, as the author of both these legal notes and my actors' dramatic dialogue, I wanted the two older women to view and listen to what I believed to be the more important scenes in the next room.

The result will be a rather chaotic dragging of mother and Laura, by their sleeves, out of this kitchen and into the improvised proscenium in the parlor. After my cast completes the important scene, I shall return them to the kitchen whereby they may continue with their legal strategy planning, and I will continue my legal transcription duties. Thus, these legal notes, by necessity, will also include the description of my play's better scenes.

In my mind, the attorneys will have the best of both worlds, even though they may not agree. Their minds, I am sad to say, are too riveted upon the rather heartless process of "building a good case." Whereas, as a dramatist and actress, my awareness is always focused upon the romantic and tragic-comic reality of "creating a staged masterpiece." The problem ensues when the constraints of money and time force me, Trella Evelyn Foltz, to use my family as the impromptu, albeit necessary, *tour de force*. I notice I have just made a pun of which Laura "de Force" Gordon will pay little heed. But I digress.

It is fortunate for me to have taken shorthand, as these notes have been clarified after having been jotted down hastily in minimized script. As a result, I do not include ornate descriptions of people and settings, as would befit, say, a novel; but I do hope to render the interchanges and dramatic dialogues with fairly accurate detail.

As with any playbill, I shall endeavor to provide a cast of

characters:

Kitchen Characters
Mrs. Clara Shortridge Foltz, Esquire (38)
Mrs. Laura de Force Gordon, Esquire (49)
Trella Evelyn Foltz (21)

Parlor Characters in the original comedy, *Water*
Matron Mermaid and Merman, Ah Toy (59)
Shark, Samuel Cortland Foltz (19)
Puffer Fish, Bertha May Foltz (17)
Flying Fish, David Milton Foltz (16)
Sardine Fish, Virginia Knox Foltz (11)

In the kitchen, we have Clara Foltz seated, her files spread out in front of her like an oriental fan, her gaze riveted upon her friend and fellow barrister's face. Mrs. Gordon, it is noted, has no files at her disposal, as she is still collecting discovery evidence and interviewing potential witnesses in her criminal case. They have returned from battle, two hardened soldiers who have surveyed their opposition, interviewed their clients and possible witnesses, and returned to meet. In the war, Captain Lees and Clara's former husband, Jerimiah, would have called their meeting "legal reconnaissance."

LAURA: My client, Mrs. Fulbright, as you know, is Chinese. Woo Changying. Customs and the Chinese Inspector were already trying to fine her and get her deported. [*with anger*] I refuse to be intimidated! I ordered her to be unshackled and to have her cell cleaned. I have already contacted the authorities.

CLARA: It seems your criminal case is tame. My civil case, on the other hand, has become supernaturally chilling. Do you recall the coyote's howl we heard when Mr. Farmer was leaving this morning? [*leans forward*] One of my witnesses, Mrs. Crutchfield, told me a rather ghastly tale about seeing Penelope Farmer appearing, first dressed and looking exactly like her mother, and then transforming into a wild coyote. We heard the same howl at the

Farmer mansion, and then the lights were extinguished.

LAURA: You can't fool me. This story has some other ramifications. What are they?

CLARA: [*sighing*] According to Navaho legend, two evil Earth people in the Glittering World must die for each holy skinwalker who dies. Penelope, whose tribal name is Dezba, and her mother, Haseya, supposedly, were holy skinwalkers. They protect the tribal law, and they can avenge it—even in death.

LAURA: Could my client be a target of value?

CLARA: I don't know. I am going to ask Adeline Quantrill. As you recall, she was able to channel the essence world in the case of the spiritualist murders. I hope she might do it again.

Ah Toy has appeared in the kitchen doorway. She beckons us to visit the parlor for a key scene in my play. I get up from my chair, grab onto my mother's arm, at the elbow, and escort her toward her rendezvous with entertainment. Although Laura Gordon is frowning, she follows us.

I can see by my siblings' positioning that they're at the beginning of the first act, scene two. The fish characters have already been introduced, and the "Wise Old Matron Mermaid," played by Ah Toy, enters the scene.

I must admit that because this is a "dry run" of *Water* my thespians are not wearing the colorful ichthyic costumes I envisage them wearing in the theater production. To compensate, the ones playing fish are mouthing words with their cheeks puffed out, in fish form, and they keep their human arms close to their torsos, waving fingers at their sides to replicate fins.

MATRON MERMAID (Ah Toy): [*floats by the others and stops*] Good morning, everyone. Are you enjoying the water today?

SARDINE FISH (Virginia): Water? What is that?

MATRON MERMAID (Ah Toy): [*smiles, and waves her hand around*] Why, water is what surrounds all of us. You are swimming in it.

SHARK (Samuel): Aha! So, water is the free and open competition I love so much. Progress always results when individuals follow their own self interests.

SARDINE FISH (Virginia): That depends. To which school do you belong? My school sees safety in numbers.

PUFFER FISH (Bertha): [*inflates cheeks*] No, water allows me to be the best fish in the sea. And if you do not like my grandiosity, you will feel my piercing barbs! [Bertha wears her moussed hair spiked in pointy, reddish-brown tendrils]

FLYING FISH (David): [*spreads his arms like wings and glides all around*] One time, I leapt into a hard, deep, and dark place where I could not breathe. Ten tentacles like the Matron has, threw me back into the sea. Is this sea called water?

MATRON MERMAID (Ah Toy): Yes! You are swimming in it. You are all protected by her, your mother, the ocean water. She feeds you, gives you life, and you must respect and obey her rules.

SHARK (Samuel): [*swims over to the mermaid, opens his mouth wide, showing his sharp teeth*] Who are you to tell me what to worship? In my world, there are no rules except what I desire. You are not a fish. You are not a woman. You are not free in this water, as you call it. You are not even human. Why should we believe you? I think I should make a good meal of you!

I add my authorial voice to conclude the scene, "The other fish look at each other, not knowing what to do. Do they attempt to protect the Matron Mermaid? Do they allow the shark to have his way?"

I take my mother and Laura by their hands and lead them back into the kitchen. They smile at me and sit back down. I pick up my notepad, ready to write.

"That was quite dramatic, Trella," my mother says, furrowing her eyebrows. "But you say it's a comedy?"

Again, my mother has jumped to conclusions about my artistic creations.

"I just wanted to establish the characters and add some tension. Comedy arises best when you can get your audience emotionally aroused. Then, the comedic scenes relieve this tension." I turn toward Laura. "Can you understand what I mean?"

She smiles, and her need to give a counter-argument to her constant rival gets the best of her, I suppose.

"Quite right. I can even see how the water mermaid, Ah Toy, can symbolize women's struggle to be a guardian to Nature, her children, and her bounties. And yet, she still must not lose her integrity as a half woman. Was this what you were trying to say?"

I was amazed at Laura's insight. As with most artists, I become transfixed at critics who can see the depth in a work you simply allowed to flow out of you.

CLARA: We must return to our discussion of our separate trials. I have been reading that the prosecution is being manipulated by the American Medical Association. They've sent Dr. Storer to be their ambassador against abortion.

LAURA: Yes, in fact, I was thinking about using Adeline for my own purposes. If she could read this doctor's mind, I could better prepare my case's arguments.

"I shall ask Samuel to inquire as to his fiancée's services at present. For all I know, they might have commercialized her talents by now." I laughed, but my mother did not take kindly to my humor.

CLARA: Family should never have to pay for favors! Haven't I instructed you well enough?

"Yes, mother. We artists have a difficult time taking anything seriously, weren't you aware?" I tossed my hair back, in my best Sarah Bernhardt impersonation.

LAURA: Once again, it seems that our sober legal world has been invaded by mysticism, witchcraft and vengeful spirits. Although, I want to scream every time I think about Dr. Storer believing that the moment a sperm fertilizes an ovum, a human being with legal rights magically appears. If that's not witchcraft, I am not a witch.

CLARA: Indeed. I also find it quite ironic that he is willing to cure a woman of her hysterical mental illnesses by surgically removing her ovaries. Without ovaries, how does she exercise the only important legal right she now owns? Procreation.

"Mother, tell me more about how these skin-waking spirits function." I was thinking of possibly adding this kind of supernatural element to my play.

CLARA: [*turns to glare at the transcriber*] Skin*walker*, my dear. Please pay attention. And correct your mistakes during the final draft.

"Yes, I shall. How can these skinwalkers kill humans? Adeline told us spirits cannot harm creatures directly."

LAURA: Oh, my goodness. Here we go again. Into the realm of Lady Shelley and her *Frankenstein* romance.

CLARA: [*raises her nose in haughtiness*] These spirits, according to Navajo legend, do *not* contact humans directly. They use a powder to sprinkle upon us.

LAURA: [*gleefully claps her hands*] Is it made from the fertility god Pan's horns? Do we, at least, die a happy death?

CLARA: [*frowns*] Quite the opposite. Their poison is made from human skeletal ash. You veered away from *Frankenstein* when you should have continued along that same line of reason. [*giggles*] Do not fear. We women, even in spirit, do not harm each other.

Unbeknownst to the two attorneys, two fish from the parlor have clandestinely swum into the kitchen. One, the youngest (sardine) is poised to attack, crouched over, her arms raised, a grim look of determination on her glowing face. She is awaiting the nod from her older compatriot-in-terror. Puffer stands behind my mother, her arms also raised, talons protracted. She nods, and they dive together, each one wrapping summer-tanned arms around the torsos of the adult women, trapping them in the chairs. The giggling is the only refraction from their murderous intent.

Ah Toy is again at the doorway leading out into the dark confines of the staged comedy. This time, she wears one of Samuel's suits. Bowler hat, black tweed britches, white shirt, bow tie, and sack coat.

AH TOY: Our creator bids you back into the limelight once more. We are prepared to show you a snippet from our final scene.

I follow the Master Merman into the parlor, and I can hear the footsteps of the two other actors and their hostages behind me. The Asian furniture and statues seem to cast eerie, warped shadows all over the youngsters as they take their positions. The sunlight streams through the long, bay window's crimson curtains, and the resulting red glow bathes their physiques in its special *Feng Shui* energy.

The Master Merman sits on the red and gold couch, her back ramrod straight, her stare vacant and without emotion. She is closely surrounded by Puffer Fish, Flying Fish and Sardine Fish. They all face the tall and ravenous Shark, each in his or her most threatening stance. As he gives his soliloquy, the Shark glides, back and forth in the water, getting closer and closer as he does so.

SHARK: [*snapping his teeth*] So, you think you can stop the Survival of the Fittest by dressing as a man? Do you believe you have the cunning and hypocrisy of humanity? Water is meant to be used by those who can survive by killing, and you are just a juicy morsel for these jaws.

PUFFER FISH (Bertha): [*inflates cheeks*] You will have to go through me first. My spiny skin will protect her. She can be any gender or creature she chooses to be.

SARDINE FISH (Virginia): If you devour me, thousands more will come to replace me. The waters give me the freedom to reproduce and grow in abundance.

FLYING FISH (David): And I am not of the water at all. In fact, I am from the Piscis Volans constellation above us. You may call me Volans. When I touch the Matron of our waters, she will become impervious to your laws of cruelty and survival.

SHARK: Impervious? Your creature's blood will flow like Vesuvius! [*swims in to attack, teeth barred, snapping viciously*]

The three fish encircle the Shark and begin to spin him, as a top, until his tall body is thrashing about helplessly. Flying Fish then jumps upon the Shark's back, and they race across the parlor, to the stairs, and they trudge upward, into the far reaches of the cosmos, to the Volans constellation. The other fish, and the three humans in the audience begin to applaud, the water encircling them with its calm flow of pacific fulfillment.

"Thank you, my friends and family. You have now had a brief baptism into my play, *Water*. I pray you will be able to attend the full production after the two trials have run their legal gametes. Shall we adjourn once more to the kitchen?" I wave to my mother and Laura, and they are smiling. They follow me, chatting together, into the kitchen.

Once seated, it is my mother who responds to my word play.

CLARA: Legal gametes? Nicely stated, Trella. I do indeed feel like an unfertilized ovum, a gamete. And you, Laura? Do you feel like a diploid as yet? Eventually, with God's grace, we can both become zygotes.

LAURA: [*laughs*] Most certainly! I know our courtrooms shall be filled with zygotes. Shark zygotes, sardine zygotes, mermaid and merman zygotes. And, naturally, the press flying and puffery zygotes.

CLARA: [*turns toward the transcriber*] My dear, I did enjoy your little comedy. However, that final scene made me think you may have committed an Aristotelean *faux-pas*. A deus ex fishery, if you will.

I know I said I would not use description, but I must state that my face became quite flushed, at this point, with anger.

"It was supposed to be funny, mother! You know, ha ha? I plan to have Samuel and David Milton mechanically raised up into the rafters of the theater. He is, after all, a magical flying fish."

CLARA: I see. Well, that explains it. [*turns back toward Laura*] I suppose our magical flying fish is Adeline, is she not?

They both laugh, and I can't help but believe it may be at my expense.

LAURA: Don't you think you should report what you have learned to Captain Lees?

CLARA: You were always the skeptic about the paranormal. What could I do to convince Isaiah to believe in these skinwalkers? Even if I hear from them through Adeline, I am not certain that I can believe it.

LAURA: But, four possible murders? There will, most likely, be death threats made against my client and yours. You do understand what our trials will be stirring up in the community? Antipathy against the Chinese, hatred of midwives, accusations of infanticide and incest against Aloysius Farmer.

CLARA: I do understand. If we were to add mysticism to that miasma of potential threats, we would become the laughing stock of the San Francisco Police Department. No, we must keep our spiritualist investigation private. Just the way Spiritualism has been the private refuge of our Suffrage Movement all these years.

LAURA: As I shall have the meager wages presented to me as a defense attorney, are you still working toward that idea about having a state-supported public defender office? It would be quite proper to be able to do adequate discovery for these poor clientele.

CLARA: Most certainly. In point of fact, I plan to use the money from Mr. Farmer's case to work on my plan and to draft the rudimentary outline. I may even present it to the Bar Association Review.

LAURA: If you need my help, please let me know. As it stands, I shall have one key witness in my case. I have already called him, and he agreed to testify on Mrs. Fulbright's behalf.

CLARA: I can ask the Woodhull ladies as well. They can provide a wealth of expertise as to the contemporary hardships women must face in marriage and in life. Who is this expert?

LAURA: Mr. Oliver Wendell Holmes Jr., Associate Justice of the Massachusetts Supreme Judicial Court. His 1884 majority opinion in re *Dietrich v. Inhabitants of Northampton* speaks directly to my manslaughter case. Since the proximate cause of the abortion was probably the girl's ectopic pregnancy, and not the acupuncture, the judge will testify how his rationale in *Dietrich* shows that the fetus cannot be a person.

CLARA: There were two victims, however. What have you to say about the death of Penelope Farmer?

The front door chimes ring. I get up from my task to answer it. A young suited clerk from San Francisco City Hall is there. He says he has a notice from the judge who will be docketing Laura's case. I escort him into the kitchen, he hands the envelope to Laura, bows, and exits.

Laura opens the envelope, reads its contents, frowns, and stares at Clara.

CLARA: Well, what is it?

LAURA: It's from Judge Frederick Lattimore. The District Attorney, Mr. Stonehill, has announced another key witness. Dr. Liu

Wei, Chief Acupuncturist, and Mrs. Fulbright's supervisor. He was in the house when Penelope Farmer made her accusation against her father and then died under Mrs. Fulbright's treatment. This means he will be showing the jury how her procedure can lead to a miscarriage and the death of both the mother and child.

CLARA: Oh, my goodness. Perhaps you can get another experienced acupuncture doctor to rebut his expertise?

LAURA: Not an acupuncturist who was in the room when the victims died. Justice Holmes's testimony might be able to address the death of the fetus, but not Penelope Farmer's death. What can I do?

CLARA: You must search for an intervening cause. Something this child may have done before she came to the clinic to be treated by Mrs. Fulbright.

"Perhaps she took a potion. You said she was a tribal witch or skinwalker, correct?" I wanted to help our friend Laura.

LAURA: [*snaps her fingers*] Of course! Thank you, Trella. I shall take a trip out to Arizona territory to visit the Navajo reservation. I want to learn as much as I can about their religion before my case goes to court next month. Can a native be sworn as a witness in our courts?

CLARA: Yes. The civil rights of the tribes were given in the case of *Standing Bear versus Crook* in 1879. It was a federal case that could not be appealed, and it bestowed all the rights of the Fourteenth Amendment to our native tribes. It led to the Dawes Act of early this year.

LAURA: Yes. I remember that President Cleveland signed that act. If I can get what information I need, I shall subpoena the Navajo Medicine Man to testify in my client's defense.

CLARA: What I find most ironic is the fact that both of our defense strategies will involve the rights of Natives, the Chinese medical community, the orphan asylums of California, and the business interests of a man who provides abortifacients in the mail to poor women. Once again, we women are left in the lurch. We have no civil rights other than being pretty little homemakers to the men who have crafted our imprisonment so diabolically as to keep the system, and the very courts where we argue, under their direct control.

LAURA: I, for one, shall not shirk from raising the specter of Women's Suffrage. If my client had been a man, she would have been permitted to become a doctor of medicine and not a lowly midwife. She would not be subjected to mistreatment in jail and the harassment by the immigration authorities. My jury, even though they are going to be all males, shall hear this, and my argument's relevance will be made crystal clear so that even a man can understand it.

I can see by the clock in the kitchen that it is four in the afternoon. The front door chimes ring. I know who it is.

"I am getting quite giddy from all of these female hormones being unleashed at once. My new boyfriend, Terrance Saylor, a fellow drama student, and I, shall now depart with the Shark, brother Samuel. You do recall, mother, that your son and Miss Quantrill are soon to be married?" I stand up, stretch my arms out wide, and yawn.

This is the last I am writing in this document. I shall leave my mother's rejoinder vacant at this point. You can well imagine what she said to me. We gametes are such frivolous beings, are we not?

Chapter 6: Head of the Earth Woman

Navaho Mountain, Navajo Nation Reservation, Coconino County, Arizona and Utah Territories, June 28, 1887.

Dr. Andrew McFarland explained the history of the Navajo tribe to Laura during their journey to visit the medicine man in Arizona. McFarland was an amateur cultural anthropologist, like his psychoanalyst hero, Dr. Sigmund Freud of Austria. He informed her that Freud was presently studying different cultures and their myths, especially as they interpret dreams, which is one of the major jobs of the shaman or medicine man or woman. Laura was quite interested, as she wanted to establish a possible intervening cause in the death of Penelope Farmer.

He began by reading her the oral creation legend of the Navajo people. She watched the passing scenery from out of their Southern Pacific dining car window. The Painted Desert was awash with color. The gray and red bands across the hills seemed to match the "four worlds" Dr. McFarland was describing as he read to her:

According to the Navajo creation story, the first world was small and pitch black. There were four seas and in the middle an island with a single pine tree existed. Ants, dragonflies, locusts and beetles lived there and made up the Air-Spirit People of the first world.

Each of the four seas was ruled by one supernatural being, the Big Water Creature, the Blue Heron, the Frog and White Thunder. Above the sea there was a black cloud, a white cloud, a blue cloud and a yellow cloud. The female spirit of life lived in the black cloud while the male spirit of dawn lived in the white.

When the blue and yellow clouds came together, the First Woman was formed, while the black and white came together to form the First Man.

The First Woman saw the light of the First Man's fire and tried to reach him three times before she finally found his home. He asked her to live with him and the First Woman agreed.

The Great Coyote was formed in water and came to the First Man and First Woman, telling them he was hatched from an egg and knew all the secrets of the water and the skies. Shortly after, second coyote appeared named First Angry, who brought witchcraft into the world.

The next part of the Navajo creation story involves the First Man, First Woman, First Angry and the coyote born in the water climbing into the second world, followed by all other creatures.

When they got to the second world, they found other beings living there, including various types of birds. A swallow welcomed them and they lived in harmony together for twenty-three days until one of the Air-Spirit People tried to sleep with the swallow chief's wife. The swallow chief found out and banished the newcomers who traveled to the third world.

In this Navajo legend, the third world is called the Yellow World and was home to six mountains, where the holy people lived. These holy people were immortal and traveled by following rainbows. There was the Talking God, Black God, Water Sprinkler and House God.

In this world First Woman gave birth to a set of twins, who were neither male nor female. Four days later, a second set of twins were born, a male and female and after twenty days, five pairs of twins had been born.

The mountain gods each took a set of twins, teaching them how to pray and wear masks before returning them to their parents. Over the next eight winters, the twins found mates and brought many people into being.

The people came into the fourth world before the sun and moon were created. They were on an island with high cliffs in the middle of a bubbling lake. With help from the Wind God, people were able to leave the island. First Man and First Woman built the first hogan to live in.

Laura found the story very comforting. In fact, the entire myth made her think about her own life and how shallow it had been, especially after having discovered that her husband, Dr. Charles

Gordon, was a bigamist, in 1878. After twenty years of marriage, she divorced him when his first wife in Scotland sent a private investigator to San Francisco to track him down. Like Clara's former husband, Jerimiah, Charles was a philanderer. Also, like Clara, Laura initially was not a lawyer or even a feminist. She first made her money as a Spiritualist, channeling the souls from the afterlife in Pennsylvania, where she was born, and in Boston. It was a profitable trick while she practiced it. Many families had lost loved ones in the war, and they were ready to believe there was a way to contact them, even if it required a spiritual conduit. When she married the physician, Dr. Gordon, in 1862, they eventually made their way out West.

Laura became a journalist and eventually became the first California woman publisher in Stockton, California. She met Clara in 1880. She was also a publisher, as they were both speaking for Women's Suffrage, and Laura became the San Francisco President of their local group for Women's Rights. However, despite the accolades from the male-dominated California legislature, when she and Clara successfully got a bill passed that allowed women to attend law school and practice law and any other profession for which they qualified, Laura still felt unfulfilled as a woman.

After she and Clara became practicing lawyers, she won most of her cases as a defense attorney. She was one of only two female attorneys appointed to argue at the Federal Supreme Court level. All of these achievements became mute after she got her divorce. In fact, in 1879, she donated a book she authored, *The Great Geysers of California and How to Reach Them*, to a 100-year Time Capsule being buried in San Francisco's Washington Square. In this book she wrote, "If this little book should see the light after its 100 years of entombment, I would like its readers to know that the author was a lover of her own sex and devoted the best years of her life in striving for the political equality and social and moral elevation of women."

Secretly, she wondered if her sexual attraction was actually for her own sex. She did not date men anymore, as she was too busy with her law practice, and the money was still scarce because the

State did not pay women as much as men. These thoughts about her private love life made her even more depressed, especially after she saw Clara's young son, David Milton, having so much trouble with his own sexual identity the previous year.

After Dr. McFarland completed his reading, she was thinking about how the Navajo had made their existence so much simpler.

Instead of worshiping each acre, the way the indigenous peoples did before we were here, we, the conquering races, chose to collect around our technologies and our buildings, all these monuments to greed and impatience. Why have we sped things up and devoured so much in so little time? Why do we lie to each other about there not being Laws of Nature, the bible of the natives, which must be obeyed to survive beyond any trumped-up legal maneuvers we create or complex political philosophies we preach? Why didn't we listen to them? These holy people were immortal and traveled by following rainbows, while we were always looking for the pots of gold at the end of those rainbows.

As if he were reading Laura's mind, Dr. McFarland looked over at her and tapped on the book he had been perusing.

"Most aborigines did not use nouns to speak. They do not need to objectify their surroundings because, to them, their surroundings are part of their own nature, their very own being. So, they use verbs." His voice was filled with reverence.

"Why?" She turned from the window to face him.

"Because Nature is action, not staid, formal, oblivious and status-seeking greed. Only giant, immovable structures, like banks and offices, can hold our greed. In a teepee or a hogan, everything is near the constant flow of life. Life is not the view one can see from twenty stories up. Life must be on the same level we are, so we can take care of it, each and every second of our existence. The golden rule for the native is to give back more to nature after you take from it. Be certain that the wheel of life can continue into the next season, by taking care of nature now."

"That's very lovely, Andrew," she told him, and she sighed. "Very Noble Savage, of you. But these natives also have their dark side, do they not? Isn't that why we're here?"

"Of course. The medicine man we shall see, Hástin Yázhe, was the one who treated Haseya, Mrs. Farmer. If anybody can help us discover what happened on that day, he can." Dr. McFarland pointed out the car window. "We've come to the depot. Let's have the porter get our bags and put them on the means of transport out to the Navajo Mountain Lodge."

The wind was warm as she stepped out of the train car, and she had read about the variety of flora and fauna from a guidebook she purchased at the Trading Post back at Fort Defiance. This was a desert land with cacti, serpents, porcupines and coyotes. It was so dry that it required irrigation to raise the corn, beans, horses, goats, wild turkeys and sheep, which were their main sustenance.

They rode on a buckboard pulled by a mule and driven by an old Navajo named Ahiga. He explained that he was educated to speak English after the Long Walk, in 1864, to the Bosque Redondo reservation in New Mexico. He called it "The Fearing Time." Around his forehead, he wore a blue kerchief tied in a knot at the back. His green velvet shirt had no collar, and his deerskin breeches and moccasins were sewn by hand. In his sixties, Ahiga's weatherworn face had valleys of dark wrinkles, but he smiled often, and he pointed out different sights along the route.

Dr. McFarland explained that the Long Walk to which Ahiga referred was very similar to the Trail of Tears for the Natives in the Southeast.

"Some eight thousand five hundred men, women and children were marched almost three hundred miles from northeastern Arizona and northwestern New Mexico to Bosque Redondo, a desolate tract on the Pecos River in eastern New Mexico at Fort Sumner. Traveling in harsh winter conditions for almost two months, about two hundred Navajo died from cold and starvation. More died after they arrived at the barren reservation."

She was horrified. "Who did that? And why?"

"The usual push West inspired by the Homestead Act. The Army of the 1860s, already girding up for the Civil War, used their battle-hardened troops to fight the Navajo and Apache. The cattle ranchers, especially, detested the Navajo because they kept herds of sheep and goats, acquired from the Spanish and Mexicans, which took grazing land away from them. Until the Treaty of Bosque Redondo, in 1868, the Navajo had fought to preserve their land against the Spanish, the Mexicans, and the United States. The Navajo lost more than two-thirds of their population, during those war years, which led to genetic diseases, such as Xeroderma Pigmentosum, due to in-breeding."

She covered her mouth with both of her hands. "Oh, my God! Is that the skin cancer disease?"

"Yes, and it afflicts the children the most. Can you imagine? Their entire culture was built upon being out-of-doors, and then the sunlight became their enemy." Dr. McFarland shook his head.

"Homesteaders are nothing," Ahiga said. "Dawes has made us enemies to each other."

Dr. McFarland nodded. "He knows what that bill has done to his people. It began with the railroads obtaining plots of reservation land during the transcontinental push. It was called checker boarding. But when President Cleveland signed the Dawes Act, it began to split the tribes apart all around the country."

"Clara was telling me about that law when we were in Washington. The government wanted to sell the land privately, to individual natives, correct?"

"Yes, but in exchange, the natives had to lose their tribal affiliation and culture. It was the only way they could become U. S. citizens."

Ahiga spat into the warm desert wind as he turned the mule toward the mountain seen in the distance under dark nimbus clouds.

"We call them *leetsoh*. Rats. They eat our grain, live on our land, but they are not welcome."

"The lodge we are going to moved away from these rats so they can maintain their tribal way of life. They are located at the base of Navajo Mountain." Dr. McFarland pointed at the edifice.

"No. *Naatsisaan*. Head of Earth Woman. She give birth to Monster Slayer. Monster Slayer stood between his holy people in the third world and Kit Carson to save them from destruction. We say those who lived the Long Walk were saved by Monster Slayer born on the sacred mountain. I am saved." He raised his fist up toward the mountain. "I am spared! I am spared! Enemy has missed me! Enemy has missed me! Today it did not happen! Today it did not happen!"

As they drove slowly toward the mountain, she began to realize the beauty, courage and grace deep within the hearts of these Navajo people. They had survived both the wrath of Man and the wrath of Nature, and yet they understood that the Earth was still their creator and master.

She saw that those thunder clouds meant business, as they passed what their driver said was the Rainbow Bridge. It was taller than the new Statue of Liberty in New York harbor, and it was created by thousands of years of erosion and winds. The red rocks, buttes, and mesas were shaped in many human and animal forms, and they were all around them inside this canyon. She could smell the piñon and sage mingle with the waves of hot winds coming up through the gorge. Dr. McFarland said they were now on the Utah territory side. The Many Sheep clan they were visiting was on the Arizona territory side.

"Hástin Yázhe is a Road Man," said their guide, as he came up to the long, communal hogan built into the side of mountain under an overhanging ledge. The rain was coming down in misty sheets, with most of it evaporating at lower elevations. The thunder and white lighting were unnerving, however, and she kept thinking about Penelope and her mother. This land and its people were so different from life inside a cold mansion in San Francisco.

"What is a Road Man?" She was surprised that Dr. McFarland didn't know that, as he was very informed about most of the Navajo and their religious rituals and ceremonies.

"He was boy who was with me on Long Walk. Mescalero already at Bosque Redondo. Their medicine man sang Peyote songs. Many people were dying from sickness. Bad water with poor food.

Hástin Yázhe learn songs. This day he sing Peyote songs from sundown to next morning. Children in boarding school. Bad medicine. Parents need to heal."

"Peyote? That was the drug the doctors secretly used on the patients in the Stockton State Insane Asylum. They wanted to create their psychotic visions to control them."

"Not control. The holy people must cry in the Enemy Way." Ahiga opened the deerskin curtain to allow Laura and Dr. McFarland entry into the hogan. It was much cooler inside, and the room was lit with standing torches on each side of the room. Wood paneling covered the inside of the mud walls connected by a frame made of pine tree planks and poles. There were about fifteen people in a circle, and the men wore native dress similar to their guide. The women had diamond and arrow patterned blankets, worn like ponchos, with a circular hole cut in the center for their heads.

She watched the man in the center, beneath the smoke hole in the roof, who held the large gourd that must have held the peyote potion. The ceremonial gourd was decorated with beads, silver, and turquoise medallions. She could smell juniper berries wafting from the heated kettle on the fire.

Hástin Yázhe wore a yellow velvet top adorned with a long silver squash blossom turquoise necklace with a *najahe,* pincer-shaped, silver ornament at the bottom. She had seen one of these necklaces in the silversmith catalogue back at the trading post in Fort Defiance, where their train had stopped for a rest.

His headdress was made from the entire body of a coyote, the head's upper jaw, teeth, and empty eye sockets forming around his long black hair, which hung down over his shoulders. The animal's gray back fur and four legs also hung over the singer's back and chest. He was a tall man, barrel-chested, in his early forties, and as soon as Ahiga spoke to him in sign language and pointed at them both with his pursed lips, in the Navajo manner, he walked toward them.

"My friends, it's so wonderful to see you! How was your trip?" The deep lines in his forehead rose with his smile, as the sun rose with the dawn. She was very surprised at his excellent English, and then she remembered the dossier she read on him. Although he was born and raised in the Navajo tribe, and he was of the Many Sheep clan, he was also a college graduate.

After being forced by the Bureau of Indian Affairs to attend boarding school, after the Long Walk to Fort Sumner, a teacher from Australia saw that he was extremely bright. As a result, he was given an exceedingly rare scholarship, to Oxford, England's most prestigious university, where he graduated with honors in 1867. He majored in Medicine and Religious Studies. However, he decided to return to his people and help them retain their culture. When Aloysius Farmer met Haseya, on the reservation in 1870, he helped her transition into the white man's world.

Hástin Yázhe sat down on a flat boulder outside the hogan and motioned for them to be seated on two others. After the thunderstorm, the sky had a brilliant rainbow arching above them toward the mountain. The medicine man stared at it as Dr. McFarland and Laura stared at him. It was as if he were transfixed in another world.

She decided to get to the heart of the matter. "We are here for a very specific purpose. We were told you were summoned when Mrs. Aloysius Farmer became ill from consumption eight years ago. You also brought her remains back with you after she died. I am afraid her daughter, Penelope, has also died at the hands of a Chinese midwife, who is now being prosecuted for manslaughter. I am an attorney representing this midwife, and I need to know what happened when you treated Haseya."

"I have studied your ways, and that is why I am here. The Holy People have been pushed into a spiritual corner. For example, these peyote songs are my way to purge my people of the sadness and depression they feel. It is not taken to see visions. My potion has a very low dosage of psychoactive ingredients. It contains only enough for these parents to feel their emotions again. Their children are being stolen from their hogans to live at the government boarding schools, learn the government's rules, and forget the ways of their ancestors."

She could see that Dr. McFarland was interested, even though the medicine man had failed to answer her question.

"I am also a medicine man. My degree is in the study of the mind, and I can see why you would want your people to feel again. What did you tell Haseya when she married Mr. Farmer?"

When Hástin Yázhe turned from the rainbow, which had faded into the sunset, to look at Dr. McFarland, she felt ignored.

"I did not tell her anything. Niyol Begay was her father. He, too, was a singer. His clan, the *Azeetsoh diné*, or Big Medicine People, has many witches and *yee naaldooshii*, or skinwalkers. Farmer did not know this, as he was too filled with his own lust to care who she was or from which clan she came. Like many of your tribe, he knew what he wanted, and he found a way to get it."

"My legal partner, Clara Foltz, told me about them. She said they protected the tribe. Did Penelope and her mother become skinwalkers after Mr. Farmer began to change? A coyote appeared to both of them. Mrs. Foltz and I also heard its howl at our residence."

He finally turned toward her. His black eyes were heavy-lidded and looked fatigued. She wondered if he took any of his own peyote potion.

"Are you familiar with Shakespeare's play *Hamlet*?" He was using this as a teaching moment, and she felt irritated.

"Yes," she nodded. "Prince of Denmark."

"The ghost of the king appears to his clan in order to protect his heritage. He had been murdered by his brother to steal both the crown and the wife. A skinwalker does the same work. It avenges the clan and its heritage. Except, instead of the simple use of a human form, our *yee naaldooshii* can transfer from human to animal, and back again. This makes them much more dangerous."

"In what way? Hamlet went mad, and so did Ophelia." She was intrigued, as she was thinking about how Haseya could have taught her daughter the ways of the skinwalker.

"After I treated her for her breathing sickness, Haseya told me about her husband turning." His brows furrowed. "When her mother died, her spirit entered Dezba, her daughter."

71

She suddenly realized she had a chance to show this in a way that could be legally acceptable to the jury at her client's trial. All she needed to know were a few additional facts. As she was about to ask the medicine man, a young squaw entered their enclave holding one of the torches to add some light to their discussion. Laura had never seen such a beautiful woman. She could not take her eyes from her as she stood holding the torch.

"Ajei cannot speak. She was kicked by a sheep in the left side of her head. But she can sing. She knows only Navajo sign language. She is also a Two Spirit. *Nadleeh.*"

She stood tall and straight like a princess, and in the torchlight, Laura could see her slanted eyes. Those captivating eyes made her remember what Dr. McFarland said about the original natives coming from Asia thousands of years ago. She wore a purple one-piece dress, with a turquoise clasp at her bosom and a matching necklace hanging in two strands down the front. Around her thin waist was a silver concho belt, with an American silver dollar at the buckle, and circling her neck was a matching silver dollar choker. Her black hair was unbridled, blowing softly in the warm breeze. When she saw Laura staring at her, she immediately lowered her gaze, but then, almost as quickly, raised her head slowly and smiled.

"If I might extend the Hamlet analogy a bit further, do you believe the girl's obsession to protect her tribal ways would extend to taking her own life and the life of the child she was bearing? I am actually asking both of you. Do you think she could have been insane? And, if she was insane, could it cause a physiological reaction in her body strong enough to kill her?"

Dr. McFarland turned toward her. "In my practice, and in the asylum statistics I have perused over the years, over twenty percent of deaths were said to be caused from stress exhaustion. When I examined the specifics of these cases, I discovered that the patients were suffering from delusional anxieties and manias which caused the stress leading directly to the breakdown of the body's vital organs."

Hástin Yázhe was more succinct with his answer. "In the Big Medicine clan, the skinwalkers can escape the body and move into other bodies. That is why our people never enter a hogan where someone has died. They do not want the witch to enter them."

The idea had formed in her mind. She was thrilled by its possibilities.

"Do you recall when Hamlet used an improvised drama to trick his murderer uncle into showing his fear about how he killed his brother?" She was looking at Ajei as she said this, thinking that she would make a superb Ophelia in a pantomimed, all-female version of the play.

Both men nodded.

"It is my proposition that we create such a drama in San Francisco. Clara, in fact, has several dramatists in her clan who can assist us in this endeavor. Would you both be available to perform in my little tragedy on the appointed date of my client's trial?"

"I am certainly already at your disposal, as I am also testifying in an expert capacity in Clara's civil case." She could see Dr. McFarland's smile under the wavering light of the torch.

She looked over at the medicine man. He slowly nodded his head.

"It would be my pleasure," he said, standing up. "If that's all, I need to return to complete my song. Ajei will show you both to your separate sleeping hogans."

***

As she lay on the deerskin mattress and pillow, filled with wool, it was getting very chilly, so she pulled the hand-woven blanket up to her chin, and she shivered. She could hear the many yelps and yips of the coyotes in the canyon, and she remembered the skin worn by Hástin Yázhe. Was he trustworthy? Or, like his skin, could he change in a flash of lighting to protect his tribe against her and what she represented? He, in fact, might be the most powerful skinwalker of them all.

The rustling sound she heard outside the hogan made her gasp. She sat up and stared at the deerskin curtain covering the opening. It moved, and as it was slowly pulled open, she saw her. It was the young mute woman, Ajei. Her shapely form was a dark

73

silhouette against the moon, which had risen behind her in the midnight sky.

Ajei approached her, knelt down at the edge of the mattress, and placed her hand on the edge of the arrowhead blanket. Under the torchlight, she could see her smile. When the girl silently pulled up the blanket and crawled in next to her, Laura's heart began to race.

She vowed to create an important role in her legal drama for this young woman to play. The wind outside began to blow down in the canyon, as the attorney's mind relaxed for the first time in many years. The odors of dying campfires, burning sage, and mutton stew, permeated her night's experience.

She exhaled, and then she breathed in the exotic reality of this tribal woman, whose four senses were dedicated to love and attention in their active present. No need for naming objects. No need for the exchange of money. Only a sensory devotion to a middle-aged attorney with a hidden, inexplicable need. She understood what "Two Spirit" meant.

Chapter 7: Scarlet Sisters

The Toy Mansion, Fifteen Nob Hill, San Francisco, July 2, 1887.

Trella Evelyn received the request to author a "legal drama" on a postcard sent by Laura Gordon from the Navajo Nation Reservation. On the back of a colorful photo of three Navajo women weaving blankets, the attorney briefly wrote: *We are bringing home a medicine man and his assistant. I would like you to write a legal drama for me to use in my criminal trial.*

Today, the same day Laura and Dr. McFarland were arriving with their guests, she was informed by her mother that Victoria Woodhull Martin and Tennessee Claflin Cook, were also arriving from England to be counseled on their testimony in the civil trial of Mr. Farmer.

She thought her new boyfriend, Terrance Jerome Saylor, was going to be the center of attention in the family's doings, but now that this was happening, it would be like getting a word in at a three-ring circus. Having the chance to create for Laura was an honor, and she supposed it was because her mother's partner was impressed by her little comedy, *Water*.

Adeline Quantrill was supposed to be over later with Samuel. Even their impending marriage plans would have to wait. From what the attorneys told her about the sisters being former Spiritualists, there would no doubt be a séance of some kind taking place in the center ring of their Barnum and Bailey extravaganza. Thank goodness, Ah Toy had taken the three youngest children to the matinee downtown.

Trella was dusting all the furniture and artwork when the door chimes rang. She wore a suffragette's summer dress, a long purple affair of cotton, no bustle, with a matching necktie draped down the center of her ruffled white blouse.

When she opened the door, she expected to see her mother, the sisters, or perhaps even Laura and Dr. McFarland, but when she saw the beaming faces of Terrance, Samuel, and Adeline, the relief she felt caused her to sing out, "You shall all rue this day. Come in quickly. I can still hide you in the closets!"

Terrance strutted in first, and he kissed her briefly on the forehead. "Tra, la, la. Trella is in high spirits already. Methinks a game is afoot," he said, handing her his black felt Homburg.

As usual, Terry was quite dashing in his black sack coat, upturned white collar and crimson, silk puff cravat. His smile and white teeth dazzled her, and she could almost see her reflection in his black pomaded hair. She was eagerly awaiting the moment when her mother saw that she was cavorting unchaperoned about town with a Negro, before she had come out to society.

Her brother, Samuel Cortland, and Adeline were also well dressed in city clothing. She noted that Samuel was wearing the new spats he received as a gift from their mother when she returned from Washington D. C. They complemented his narrow-toed black dress shoes, gray waistcoat, matching trousers, and white shirt and tie. Adeline sported a shell bustle day dress that had contrasting stripes of red and white satin layers and a red, swan-feathered hat that she wore tilted to the side.

She followed her friends out into the parlor. They variously took up seats on the dragon couch and in one of the two stuffed chairs. She addressed them while standing next to the Goddess Mazu statue. Her mother would say it was quite appropriate.

"Adeline will be featured in tonight's meeting. As I told you earlier, I will also be getting the specifics as to what attorney Gordon wants in the manner of a courtroom presentation. Terry, since your father is also an attorney, you may be playing an important role. I trust that is acceptable?"

She could see her boyfriend was lounging on the couch, his back curled into the corner, his right arm draped over the back, staring up at her.

"Did I meet you in the school for dramatic arts? Have we not discussed this? You and I, dear Trella, are not obnoxious, single-minded barristers. We think in terms of artistic expression and the common good. However, if you are the playwright, then I shall do your bidding."

She blew him a kiss.

"Thank you for having faith in me."

She turned toward Samuel and Adeline, who were sharing one of the two stuffed chairs. "I must apologize to you two love birds. But you know how mother gets when there's a big trial on the horizon. In this case, there are two trials. Your engagement must be postponed for the good of the family Foltz."

She saw Adeline blush, but Samuel looked rather relieved.

"We understand. If she is victorious, however, our honeymoon will be that much grander," her brother said.

Adeline sat up straight and stared into space. Her eyebrows were still red smudges to affect the look of a Japanese woman of mystery. Her lips were crimson buds, and her face was powdered white, with red rouge on her cheeks. She knew that face. It was the face she always used when she was channeling a spiritual presence or perusing her autobiographical memory.

"They are both outside. I can feel their presence." Adeline spoke, her head swiveling toward the front door.

Yip, yip, yip. Yeeee-owww!

Everyone in the room turned toward the door.

She watched Terry spring up from the couch and dash over to open it.

"There's nothing out here. What was that howling?"

Trella didn't know if she should tell them about the coyotes or wait until her mother arrived. She received her answer right away.

"Wait one moment. I think I see people coming up the path near the garden." Terry craned his neck and stepped outside, and she exited the parlor to join him.

She could see the carriage cab driver toting and grunting the luggage up the walkway ahead of Dr. McFarland, Laura Gordon, her mother, and two dark-skinned persons. The broad-chested man wore an old-fashioned frock coat, with a native silver and turquoise necklace which replaced his tie, and instead of men's dress shoes, he wore moccasins. He also wore a red bandana around his forehead.

His companion, a young woman, was dressed in a complete Indian outfit, with a pleated-velvet turquoise skirt and matching long-sleeved blouse. She also wore a silver and black choker and black earrings in the shape of two crows. Her shiny-black hair was swept up into a bun and held at the back with a much larger crow barrette. Her steps were taken softly in deerskin moccasins, her black eyes were cast downward, as she followed directly behind the older man in his shadow.

She realized that this scene was becoming a mysterious comingling of ancient tribal rituals and modern Spiritualism. When the Scarlet Sisters arrived, the adventures would truly begin, so she wanted to understand what Laura wanted in the way of her plan to stage a courtroom drama.

"Welcome, Mrs. Foltz," Terry said, bowing as he extended his hand. "Terrance Saylor. I am your daughter's rival in the drama department, and my father, Albert, is also an attorney in the Estate and Income field. Your case has been the dramatic subject at our dinner table for several evenings this week. Thank you for allowing me to participate."

She noticed that her mother was not in the least chagrined by her new boyfriend's race. In typical Foltz fashion, she marched directly into the parlor to arrange the night's festivities. She began issuing orders immediately.

"On my way back from the train station to pick-up our new arrivals, I jotted down an agenda. I called Isaiah and asked him to fetch Victoria and Tennie C. at the pier. Their steamship is docking at six. We should be finished with our first phase by then."

As she spoke, her mother waved people into the back of the mansion toward the library. It was a much larger room with many chairs and a long, mahogany table. She knew Clara would be sitting at the head of that table.

Samuel hugged his mother as he entered the room. "Are you saving Adeline for later, as one saves paranormal dessert?"

"You might be the mind-reader in the family," she told him. "That is exactly what I was planning to do. Laura and I now have our respective court dates, so our preparation can begin in earnest."

She touched the elder attorney on her shoulder as she walked into the library. "Laura, we heard the coyote howling again. There were two this time."

Laura pulled two chairs out from the library table. She turned toward the Navajo guests. "Please, sit here. I shall introduce you to the others." She then turned toward Trella. "I met this Navajo medicine man in Arizona. He was wearing a coyote skin. He should be able to explain a lot about what we need to know."

After everyone was seated, Clara Shortridge Foltz, attorney at law, called the meeting to order. She watched her mother's eyes focus upon each of them, in order, as she gave the introductions.

"Ladies and Gentlemen, friends and family, I welcome you to the Toy Mansion. The owner of this home, Miss Ah Toy, will be passing by, probably as we speak, to escort my younger children upstairs. They have had a busy day in San Francisco attending the summer matinees and visiting museums. As their mother, I place great value in extra-curricular entertainment. In fact, these children have also assisted me in my own legal cases, and two of my eldest will attest to how much learning took place during those experiences."

Trella stood up. "Mother, we have learned so much that we want you to begin our instruction right away. Without further ado, I need to hear from your partner before I can bring my skills to bear."

"Quite right. This is my daughter, Trella Evelyn, whose impatience often reflects her youth. Also, my son, Samuel Cortland, is seated next to his future wife, Adeline Quantrill, whose expertise you shall be experiencing shortly." She extended her arm toward them, and they nodded their heads.

"Our guest of honor, and Navajo tribal medicine man, Hástin Yázhe, was educated at Oxford, in England, and he will be assisted by Miss Ajei. We hope to learn much from both of you."

The others at the table applauded, and Trella noticed that Laura, who was seated next to the Navajo maiden, patted her on the back and smiled at her.

Her mother looked down at her notes, cleared her throat, and raised her head.

"First on my agenda is the case which is docketed for next Wednesday, the State of California versus Fulbright. With that court date forthcoming, I will now turn it over to my legal partner, Laura de Force Gordon, who is trying this case as the defense counsel for Mrs. Fulbright. She will explain the necessary background information and what she needs in the way of cooperation from some of you."

Laura rose at her place and stared directly at her.

"Trella has agreed to author a courtroom drama for me. You should all be aware, if you are not presently, that the goal of the defense counsel is to place logical and realistic obstacles in the minds of the male jurors so that the Prosecution cannot prove his case beyond any reasonable doubt. What my opposition will try to prove is that my client, a midwife, caused the deaths of both Miss Penelope Farmer, the mother, and the fifteen-week-old fetus she was carrying. As in most homicides, the perpetration of the act comes in degrees of intent. The most serious is when the perpetrator acted with malice aforethought, or with a lethal weapon, or she harbored some hatred for the victims so that she planned the act and carried it out with no remorse or extenuating circumstances."

"Most abortion cases never go to trial under the accusation of first-degree murder because we women are too emotional and illogical to plan such deeds," her mother pointed out, in a sarcastic tone.

A few of the women snickered.

Laura nodded. "Yes, and second-degree murder requires an intentional element as well, but no premeditation. Since my client was acting in her professional capacity as a midwife, the element of my client harboring an intentional dislike or hatred for the victim is also very difficult to prove."

"But the girl was a Navajo. Perhaps your client believed we Navajos should not reproduce." She noted that the medicine man was demonstrating his Oxford intelligence.

Laura smiled. "Good thinking. However, Mrs. Fulbright is Chinese. She was willing to help Penelope when others would not. No, my plan is to show how Penelope's Navajo culture may have caused her death. As you told me at the reservation, after Penelope's mother died of consumption, her father turned. What did you mean by that?"

"He turned evil when his wife's spirit entered his daughter. I was not able to instruct the girl. She remained near the body too long."

"That's what I need to demonstrate in the courtroom. Trella? Did you get that? I want a way to question Hástin Yázhe so the jury can see that even if an actual spirit possession did not take place, it was so very real to the girl that her mind believed it *did* take place. Do you understand what I mean?"

She felt the brown eyes of the attorney bore into her, and she squirmed a bit in her chair.

"Yes. I do. I would suggest he wear his full tribal medicine man regalia when he testifies. You said the prosecution has Dr. Storer as their key expert witness. Well, then, Hástin Yázhe shall be your physician witness, so to speak. Sir, can you explain how spirit possession takes place in vivid and sensory details?"

They heard the smashing of her head on the table before they saw it. It was Adeline. She had entered one of her channeling trances. Trella could see the drool coming out of the side of her mouth. Her eyes rolled back in their sockets.

When she sprang up, Adeline's gaze was lurid and wild. She swiveled her head, back and forth, until her reddish-brown hair came loose from under her hair band and swayed together with each phrase she spoke. Her voice was that of a much older woman, and her words were in a foreign tongue. After her harangue was completed, Adeline returned to her conscious self, smiling at everyone as if nothing had occurred.

Laura was transfixed. "What did she say?"

The medicine man's voice was tentative, and its volume trembled a bit. "She said they are both outside. At this moment. The Angry Coyotes have come to avenge their deaths. Four must die to avenge them. Skinwalker witches are real, my friends. This is no drama. This is my faith."

Yip-yip-yip-yoweeeeooo!

They all heard the wailing call of the coyotes outside the mansion.

Then, the lights went out.

81

Trella screamed, and she became a believer. Who *was* going to pay for their deaths? Was she doing something bad by seeing Terry? Would they both die because of it? Perhaps it would be Laura and her new Navajo maiden. Or, Adeline and Samuel. Clara and her lover, Captain Lees. The insanity of the possibilities was entering her mind, and the courtroom drama she was supposed to invent was coming to life in her mind.

"I believe I can write it now," she said, and, as if in response, the lights dimmed, and then came back to full brightness.

The chimes at the front door rang, and they all flinched. Once more, it was her courageous boyfriend, Terry, who answered the call.

"I'll get it," he said, and they all watched him as he ran, his eyes wide and his legs stiff, out of the library and into the foyer.

"How long have the skinwalkers been here?" Hástin Yázhe was standing by the bookcase browsing at one of the titles. He pulled it out, looked inside, and shook his head. "Too many law books."

Ajei was standing next to him. Her black eyes were wide, her fingers were creating different shapes and signs in the air, and she kept poking the medicine man on his shoulder to get his attention. He turned to watch her, and then he returned to his book.

"I understand," he whispered. "But we can't go back now. They must taste the real revenge of our culture to expose their greed for our land."

Trella made a mental note of what the medicine man said. She would discuss it later with her mother and Laura. She heard the trumpets' blare at the door to the library, and, along with the others, she turned around to see what it was.

On either side of the archway entrance to the library, two women, in full Heralds' uniforms of red and gold, tiny black berets, red puffy blouses and short pants, with white tights beneath, were blowing ear-splitting notes on gold trumpets. Under each trumpet was a black and red flag, with gold trim, featuring the British medieval lion on their facing.

She watched as the heralds lowered their horns. The one on the right announced, in a notably refined English accent:

"Mrs. Victoria Woodhull Martin of London. Her Lady Tennessee Celeste Cook, Viscountess of Montserrat."

Trella had read about these two women, as they were going to be used by her mother as expert witnesses in her defense of Mr. Farmer. She found it quite ironic that most of their speeches, articles, and themes were very much in defense of the female, who needed to be independent of the patriarchal control and domination of their husbands, and yet, in their personal relationships, they had obtained their wealth from marriages that allowed them to have that freedom.

Clara spoke with an impassioned tone from her place at the head of the table. "Welcome to the Toy Mansion, ladies! Please, have a seat, and I shall continue with my agenda. We were discussing the plans for our cases, about which I have sent you the basic information. However, we were, just moments before you arrived, beset upon by a paranormal phenomenon that has suddenly made our activities very complicated."

The two sisters were clad in fire engine red satin dresses, with tiny gold emblems of royal British lion insignias covering the material like a leopard's spots. They wore no hats and no bustles, and for women of forty-nine and forty-three years of age, respectively, their hem lines reached just below their knees. Their bare-shoulders, and diamond necklaces that plunged between their breasts, made twenty-one-year-old First Lady Frances Cleveland's *avant-garde* dresses appear modest by comparison.

She knew that they became British citizens in 1877 only because they were paid a bribe by Cornelius Vanderbilt's son, William Henry, to move there. He feared they would testify in his father's legal trial over his inheritance. The elder gentleman, the wealthiest man in America, had once asked Tennessee to marry him, and he had also financed their 1871 venture to become the first-ever female Stock Brokers.

Like chameleons, it seemed the sisters easily adapted to the colors of whichever political and financial cause or country they inhabited or married into. Perhaps she could learn more about the thespian arts from these Scarlet Sisters than she was now obtaining from college.

She watched the two sisters stroll over to chairs next to Captain Lees. They smiled down at him, and by the raised eyebrows of Isaiah, she could surmise how they had been successful in their earlier years. Their animal magnetism and beauty were obviously still affecting gentlemen over fifty.

Victoria spoke once she was seated. "Thank you, Mrs. Foltz. Tennie and I have had a long voyage, and we spent much of it discussing how we could best assist you in your cases. If you need us to explain how women are being subjected to the same pitiful degradation in Great Britain and in Europe, we can do that. If you need more direct testimony about how the woman's body is the Temple of God, and how she must be treated accordingly, both in the bedroom and in public society, we can do that as well."

"Of course, we would appreciate your expertise in these matters, as we both are suffragettes. However, as we are also lawyers, subject to the legalities of a male-dominated system, the strategies we create must be planned with specific laws in mind. My partner, Laura de Force Gordon, has been more successful than I as a defense counsel, and she is confronting a most interesting dilemma. I shall allow her to explain the details and recent developments."

Laura stood up. "Before we were interrupted by what can only be described as a strangely surreal animal visitation and subsequent blackout, I was telling the group about the laws of manslaughter. My client, a Chinese midwife, is the accused, and the victim, Miss Penelope Farmer, was a sixteen-year-old half-breed Navajo."

"Her daddy was the father, right? We found this happenin' quite regular in the pitiful squalor of our industrialized cities, where families are forced by their landlords to live close together. Incest is the worst sin a family can experience." Tennessee shook her head.

She noticed the younger sister still had the Ohio twang of her youth.

"Correct. But I have found that using appeals to pity do not work on all-male juries. They, for the most part, blame the victims. This case, in point of fact, involves a wealthy entrepreneur, Aloysius

Farmer, who made his money selling abortifacients to poor women in the mail. They were not, by any means, living in a tenement hovel. They were living on Nob Hill. In this instance, I was preparing to use the Navajo beliefs of the mother to show how the girl could have become mentally affected enough to cause her own demise," Laura said.

"Aha, I see. A defense of diminished capacity. These rogues are often sympathetic to such appeals, are they not?" Victoria said.

She decided to add something also. "I was appointed to write a courtroom drama based on this occurrence. Perhaps Mrs. Cook might want to testify concerning her experiences and observations concerning incest and the supernatural? That would add special ingredients to my little play."

"Trella Evelyn is my daughter. She lives her life, like Lady Macbeth, upon a different, elevated plane. However, she is a superb writer. She can also work closely with everyone who will be testifying, so there should be some organization to this enterprise." Clara nodded at her and smiled.

"Thank you, mother. I am certainly anxious to develop an outline using the specifics of your experiences. We can, in fact, practice right here before the trials take place." She pointed toward Terrance and Samuel. "My boyfriend, Terrance, and my brother, Samuel, are certainly willing to play the prosecution, as am I."

"Four of us, as a matter of fact, have worked as publishers and authors. I would be remiss if I did not say that we plan to take advantage of the Fourth Estate being here to cover both cases. The rare opportunity to have you distinguished ladies, one of whom was a presidential nominee three times during the 1870s and 80s, can be a greet boon to our legal cause." Her mother pointed out.

Victoria Woodhull Martin laughed. "Are you certain you *are* journalists? Did you not see the cartoon by Mister Nast portraying me as the wife of Satan? My ideas about Free Love, to twist a phrase, have not enamored me to the public. Although the journalists constantly make their own definitions of what I mean, which invariably label me as a sexual libertine."

Her mother nodded. "Yes, we understand. However, as

attorneys, we know that our real audience shall be sequestered from the media after the trials begin. We need to make our *voir dire* selections very carefully, of course. Controversy is always good publicity, however, and these cases are, most certainly, controversial."

The medicine man stood up. All eyes at the table turned toward him. The Scarlet Sisters were especially intrigued at his appearance.

"I am very sorry," Laura said. "This is Mr. Hástin Yázhe. He was, quite interestingly, educated at Oxford University. However, he is now the medicine man of the Many Sheep clan in the Navajo Nation, Arizona, Utah, and New Mexico territories. He has kindly agreed to testify as an expert witness at my trial."

"My people have been backed into a corner, both physically and spiritually. I am sad to report, this sober exercise of yours has become cursed. The two women who died, Mrs. Farmer, Haseya, and her daughter Penelope, Dezba, are skinwalkers. Witches who protect my Holy People and their ways. They have returned to kill four of you. I have no control over them, I am sad to say. If you continue to drag their names and experiences in front of the glittering, Fourth World and our enemies, I cannot be responsible for what will happen as a result."

There was dead silence in the library, and it was as if their entire group had fallen into a whirlpool of poison, and the laws of the United States, no matter how well they tried to adhere to them, would never be the same again.

"I am sorry to hear that," her mother said. "Does this mean you cannot testify?"

"I never said that. In fact, I believe I am now cursed as well because Ajei has just informed me that she has slept with Laura Gordon. She was afraid she caused this curse, but I don't believe she has. I shall stay to do what you request. I will do everything I can to ward off these two witches, but I cannot promise what will happen."

"Thank you. That is all for tonight, I am afraid. I will be calling you all when we can practice. Please be very careful going home and to your hotel. May God be with us." Her mother closed the meeting, and Trella was left with a horrid chill that opened her mind to many more possibilities.

Chapter 8: Patriot Press

The Toy Mansion, Fifteen Nob Hill, San Francisco, July 4, 1887.

She was celebrating Independence Day with her own vow to become independent. Her autonomous newspaper, *The San Diego Daily Bee*, was clandestinely purchased in May of this year. In fact, Clara did not want her family to know about this acquisition or about her plans to move down to San Diego following the trial. If she won, then she would have enough collateral to move her family there. If she lost, then she would need to find other ways to get the money. Either way, she *was* going to move.

Of course, she would be leaving her friends, and this was most difficult. Her lover, Isaiah Foltz, would need to be informed, and she was keeping this from him, which would not make leaving any easier. Ah Toy had helped her in so many ways, both in her legal and detective work and with her financial problems. Ah Toy would have more time to visit than Isaiah, but her age of fifty-nine was becoming more of a factor.

It was her immediate family, however, which concerned her the most. Her parents, in their early sixties, were now living in San Jose, and they were being cared for by a nurse whose wages were paid from the stipend she sent her parents every month. Her father, Elias, still could handle their finances, but her mother, Talitha, was having frequent losses of memory and had bouts of dropsy and anxieties concerning a wide range of real and fabricated events.

The youngest of her children, David Milton, Bertha May, and Virginia Knox, would be going with her, for certain. However, Samuel Cortland was getting married to Adeline, and Trella Evelyn was finishing her studies at Berkeley. She would need to discuss their possible relocation to San Diego, but the more rural and conservative environs, she was almost certain, would not appeal to them.

The trials were coming up on Wednesday and Thursday, and she was going to meet with the Claflin sisters and Laura today to discuss their strategies concerning the media. Laura had never been a person to go to picnics or celebrate the nation's independence. She believed, along with Clara, that as long as women were subjugated to the social and legal shackles of male domination, there was no reason to rejoice on such holidays. As for the two ex-patriots from England, they lived in an affluent world of their own making. As journalists, all four of them understood this rare opportunity they had to advance women's rights and to protect their clients by utilizing the American press to their advantage.

As a result, Ah Toy and Trella Evelyn were taking the children, and the two Navajos, to picnic at Golden Gate Park, and to watch the firework display later in the evening. In the meanwhile, the four intrepid suffragettes would plan their media campaign, and Laura promised she would reveal the strategy behind her Shakespearean courtroom drama.

When the door chimes rang, she was making finishing touches to her hair, face and makeup, vaguely recalling Isaiah's comment about "women who dress for other women." She took one last look in her bedroom dressing mirror. She was no longer the young face of the mother in Iowa and Illinois, dropping children out each year like a prize rabbit. She was alone, fighting for justice, and a family that was beginning to grow out from under her.

Trella had finally convinced her to wear clothes that were modern, so she had on a ruffled, long-sleeved white blouse, with a cameo at the throat, and her skirt had no bustle and was plain brown tweed. Her boots were like Laura and all the other suffragettes wore, long and shiny, with pointed toes for kicking at the proper male appendages.

As the three women entered the mansion, she noticed they had all dressed for the Fourth of July. This was unexpected because she had never seen Laura in anything but her conservative "people's dress," the navy-blue uniform with straight skirt and no bustle. They wore the colors of both the flags of England and the United States, so perhaps it wasn't essentially Yankee patriotism. Red skirts, white blouses, and white straw hats with blue ribbons hanging from the crowns.

"Come right in, ladies. I would play Yankee Doodle on my

flute, but I let David Milton have it for the picnic." She waved them inside to the foyer and shut the door. "Shall we go inside the library once more? I have had it exorcised of skinwalkers by our medicine man since we last met." She chuckled, but when she saw no response, she followed them into the room without any more levity.

Before she could call her meeting to order, Laura was obviously up in arms about something. Her grim smile meant she had something important to relate.

"I briefly mentioned my plan to Victoria and Tennessee, to have this courtroom drama staged, so now I want to speak to you, Clara, about why and how it should be done. Since Trella will be our author, you should know what it will entail and the strategy behind its implementation."

She smiled at her friend. "By all means. Please explain," she said.

"First of all, I don't think you or I believe the death of Penelope Farmer concerns an actual revenge of evil witches, skinwalkers or spirits. If you do, then please inform me now, and explain the sane reasons why you might have such beliefs." Her dark eyes swiveled to focus upon each of the them.

When she came to her, Clara again smiled. "You should know me by now, Laura. Adeline, my son's fiancée, has forever given me a healthy respect for all things psychic and paranormal. As for this specific event, concerning Miss Penelope Farmer, no, I can't say I do believe in these Native spirits. However, we all saw Adeline's reaction, and it was not caused by anything we could see with our eyes. Was it?"

Laura slowly nodded. "Yes, I have also seen Adeline in action, and I believe in those events that we observed during the case of the Spiritualist murders. Women *can* be put into murderous trances, and Adeline *can* channel people that she has met in the past. But this is quite different."

"My sister and I are also well versed in the paranormal and spiritualist practices for many years. We have come to the conclusion that these events have one foot in this so-called real world and in another, much higher dimension. You may call it the spirit world or by any other, more scientific term, but it is still the same. It is unexplainable and incontrovertible." Victoria was quite adamant.

"With my own eyes, I saw women and men rise up from their deathbeds because they believed they could hear their kin from the afterlife, or they become entranced by the voice of an invisible angel or god. I know I didn't hold that power. I was just a medium who'd allowed 'em to hear. And, by God, they did!" Tennessee was obviously firm in her convictions as well. "Commodore Cornelius Vanderbilt was able to speak to his departed wife, Sophia, and he believed I was the one who made that happen. Faith is both a powerful conduit and a wonderful savior."

She recalled reading about Tennie's "magnetic massages." Her muscle rubs, Oriental back-walking, and the electronic jolting of the legs had invigorated the septuagenarian enough for him to rise up from his bed. And, according to reporters, she was invited into his bed to entice him into becoming a Broad Street investment tutor and financial backer to the entrepreneurial sisters. He set them up in the first-ever female stock brokerage in 1870, and it caused quite a scandal.

Laura cleared her throat. "Thank you, but I must admit, before my interview with Mr. Farmer and his household staff, I was inclined to suspect that the medicine man, Hástin Yázhe, and Ajei, his assistant, might be behind these supernatural occurrences. Why did Ajei sleep with me? Am I being manipulated?"

"I am very happy to hear you say that." She was going to tell the group about what her daughter overheard, and this was a good segue. "I can see why you might suspect them. Trella also told me what she overheard Hástin Yázhe tell Ajei during our first library meeting."

"Oh yes? Please tell us," Victoria said.

She exhaled. "She told me he whispered to his assistant that 'we,' I would assume he meant the dominant cultural pronoun, needed to experience the Navajo's revenge because of the greed we have for their land."

"That is quite logical. However, most of the problems of the natives have happened because of a divide and conquer philosophy that has worked against them. As this educated medicine man has admitted, they have been pushed into a corner and are fighting for their lives. It is my theory that some other party or person is taking advantage of this predicament in order to advance a different agenda."

"A different agenda? What do you mean?" Tennessee was curious.

Laura had a file with her on the table. She reached inside the folder and drew out a piece of paper.

"I did some research as to the newspaper coverage being done during these two trials. Most of the opinions and articles being written are about abortion and the midwives who cater to women who want to get these abortions. A few of the writings involve Mr. Farmer's mail order business selling abortifacients, but they quickly point out his *caveat emptor* warnings to women who would purchase such products and that Farmer has protected himself by placing these warnings on all of his products."

Laura folded the paper in half and tucked it back into her file.

"And so, what is your proposal?" She was anxious to get to the bottom of her partner's research. "Do you still believe Penelope caused her own demise? Wasn't it due to her Navajo beliefs?"

"The rhetorical question I asked myself is this. What would a misogynist or religious fanatic do in order to use the press as a smokescreen of disinformation?"

Victoria raised her hand. "I know. If this person knew beforehand that the Farmer women were Navajo, then he or she would use this fact as a way to distract the public from treacherous murders yet to be committed."

"My sister is correct. When she ran for President, all the press talked about was her Free Love beliefs and not her workers' and women's rights proposals. Distraction was how we lost." Tennessee pounded her right fist on the table.

She was finally seeing what Laura meant. "You believe this person was somehow responsible for Penelope's death and if you bring out her Navajo spiritual beliefs, especially the skinwalkers' curse, then you will be doing just what this person wants."

Laura exhaled. "Yes, and during this courtroom revelation, this unknown person will, quite possibly, kill innocent people to show that the Navajo witches do exist and want to take revenge on the public."

"But what if the medicine man and his assistant are, in fact, the guilty ones? Do you have definitive proof that they are not?" She leaned forward and touched Laura's sleeve. "Is it worth the risk not to pursue the possible truth of the matter?"

"Clara, you have hit upon the crux of the dilemma we now face. The truth lurks in the shadows, as we have seen before. However, we are all journalists, are we not? We can write, and we can publish our opinions," Laura said.

"Do you mean we should expose the Navajo medicine man for what he is?" She stared into her friend's dark eyes, searching for a motive.

"By the way, I already know about your purchase of the *San Diego Bee*. I do read the publishers' magazines, you know. My proposal is to author our own articles and letters to the editors about the Farmer women and their status as witches and skinwalkers. Our goal will be to prove that this is all just a sad and superstitious way these poor natives have to protect themselves from what they perceive as an encroaching danger to their culture and livelihood."

"Is it also your plan that these articles in the patriot press of yours shall bring out a response from the truly guilty party?" Victoria enquired.

"It may. Although I doubt this person will write under his or her real name. The true purpose, in my mind, is to flush this mad person out of the brush and into the air. Our shotguns must be ready to blast him asunder." It was Laura's turn to strike the table with a fist.

She grasped Laura's hands within her own and stared deeply into her eyes.

"And, so what is your plan for Trella and the criminal courtroom drama?"

"I would have a play in which our medicine man admits that

his skinwalker legend is superstitious quackery. But not before he explains it so that the audience's hair is standing straight and prickly upon their mammalian bodies in horrible fright. When I finally get the truth from him, about how he needed these two women to believe in their powers, the court and the truly guilty party will react."

She finally understood. "And if he refuses to testify in this manner? That will allow us to keep him as a prime suspect, will it not?"

"It will. Either way, we must be prepared for terror to strike. If this person caused Penelope to go insane and to die, then other lives are certainly in danger. My intuition tells me that the guilty party exists somewhere inside that Farmer mansion. One of the household staff. Perhaps an employee of Mr. Farmer or an enemy of his business, or even a friend. We must watch them all and question them all. If and when they bring about the Navajo curse, then we will have failed in our mission to protect the innocent."

She decided to take control of the meeting. "I suggest we write these missives on our own, and then we can convene to give suggestions and make alterations, if need be. I shall publish in my new periodical, and we can use the United Press syndicated wire service as well. There will be thousands of demonstrators and provocateurs attending both of these trials."

"Tennessee and I will work on those articles at our hotel," said Victoria.

She smiled at the sisters and then turned to her compatriot. "Laura, we need to discuss our jury selection strategies, in private. Also, I don't know much about Judge Lockhart, and I know you have argued before him. At our meeting, can you give me some background on him?"

"Of course." Laura made a pantomime gesture, held an invisible hangman's noose to the right side of her neck with her right fist, tilted her head to the left, and twisted her mouth into a strangulated sneer. She at once knew the general attitude of this particular judge. Not good for the Defense.

San Francisco California, Golden Gate Park, July 4, 1887.

Trella Evelyn was enjoying the picnic at Golden Gate Park. It was the first time she had been able to be with her siblings for recreation in over a year. Her schooling was taking up a lot of her time, and she was also doing legal and discovery research for her mother. Ah Toy was showing the children where the fireworks would be going off near Chinatown, and they were all meeting back at the grizzly bear pit in the children's park. She, in the interim, was escorting the Navajo visitors around the park and its environs.

Cable, electric, and steam-cars reached the park from all parts of the city, and they rode the Nob Hill cable car down California to the park built on sand in the 1870s. The entrance was on Stanyan and Haight Streets. She thought it must be quite a culture shock to these natives, even to Mr. Hástin Yázhe, who had spent four years in London. He walked ahead of her and his assistant, Miss Ajei, as if he were back in London, staring straight ahead, grim countenance, but strutting in moccasins, which was rather disconcerting to see.

The people strolling in the park wore city clothes, although she could recognize quite a few women without bustles and who were, quite obviously, making a fashion statement about suffrage, sporting long neckties and flat, unfeminine hats, just the way she attempted to do. She was happy that her mother had finally gotten into the wave of female liberty with her dresses, although she knew that on the day in court, she would be back into her highly feminine coiffure, tiny straw hat, bulging bustle, parasol, and frilly blouse.

She told them they were having their picnic in a small park near Chinatown, at Portsmouth Square, but Ah Toy, David Milton, Bertha May, and Virginia Knox were meeting them soon at the Children's Playground section of the park.

She could smell all the celebratory food delicacy booths as they walked. Fresh seafood was steaming, and the large Dungeness crabs, she noticed, were selling three for a quarter. There was the Boudin Family, serving their French sourdough bread. It smelled scrumptious as she inhaled its sweet and sour odor. Finally, up ahead, the Italian chocolate maker, Domingo Ghirardelli, was serving up squares of his famous product from Fisherman's Wharf.

The young children were being swung by nannies in the little white boats sprinkled all over the park's lush green lawns and hills, while their parents enjoyed their picnics and drank their wines on blankets nearby. Young couples in love were seated on the many benches along the major walkway, and the tall eucalyptus and palm trees waved in the sea winds.

She wished Terrance were there to accompany her, but her being seen with a Negro, even a wealthy one, on one of the major holidays, would have immediately become grist for the gossip columnists in the local newspapers. She knew that by escorting the two Navajo natives, who had already been written about in relation to the legal cases, the Foltz name was being run through the rumor mill.

However, the most outrageous story that was published was a column in the *Chronicle* by Beatrice Holcombe, who was known as the "gossip grand dame of Nob Hill," by both her supporters and detractors. Miss Holcombe had been dining at *Fior d'Italia* on Mason Street, which opened last year. While there, she observed, "Attorney Laura de Force Gordon in a booth with a Navajo woman, a witness for the defense, and they were holding hands, gazing into each other's eyes like mooning cows," was how the writer had phrased it. Laura said she was merely attempting to learn how to speak in hand sign signals to the mute woman. Their physical touching was completely misconstrued.

The other journalism pieces were about the two different cases and the key witnesses involved. Dr. Horatio Storer, Judge Oliver Wendell Holmes, and the Claflin sisters from England, were the main topics, and much speculation was given as to what would occur inside the courtrooms.

Depending upon the political sympathy of the publisher, the opinions ranged from complete condemnation to complete exoneration. The majority stated that the accused, midwife Mrs. Honora Fulbright and her "accomplice" in the civil trial, incestuous businessman and purveyor of deadly abortifacients, Aloysius Farmer, were both guilty. While in the small number of suffragette periodicals it was stated that Mr. Farmer should be the only accused criminal and civil litigant, and that Mrs. Fulbright was completely innocent in the matter and was simply "doing her duty."

She could see her siblings coming up over the hill from Chinatown. Ah Toy, in her green *cheongsam*, was leading them, holding hands with Bertha and Virginia. David Milton skipped alongside them. Thank goodness, David had not taken to wearing skirts in public, as yet, but his red gabardine trousers, white suspenders, red star-studded frilly blue shirt, and blue bowler set him off rather well from the conservative crowds around them.

"Come, children. We can see the animals and ride the elephants. Mind Virginia that she does not throw anything down into the grizzly bear pit," she commanded, rushing up to her ten-year-old sister and hugging her. "Then, when it gets dark, we can go to Chinatown and watch the fireworks. Would you enjoy that, Clara Virginia?" She nuzzled the girl's neck with her chin.

Since she was a child, a kaleidoscope of captive creatures has inhabited the park. The menagerie has included bison, deer, elk, moose, caribou, and antelope. At one time, donkeys and goats gave rides to children, while chickens inhabited an imitation barnyard, both located in the Children's Playground. More exotic specimens have included elephant, zebra, bear, kangaroo, emu, and ostrich. A spectrum of smaller unusual birds, including pheasants of many types, peacock, and quail, were all part of the park's grand landscape.

She was entranced, along with her Navajo guests, at the giant elephants and their caretakers dressed as Uncle Sam. Ajei decided to enjoy the elephant ride with the three younger Foltz children. As they rode upon the Indian pachyderms, she could see their bodies swaying inside the gondola saddles, their eyes bright and wide, as they gazed around at the lush trees and bountiful vegetation. She knew their minds, like hers before, were filled with the enchanted dreams of childhood. In one's imagination, she believed, all the world and its cultures could come together to enjoy the exotic members of their various communities.

After an hour of visiting and petting a variety of species, one of which, an angry Bantam rooster, pecked Virginia Knox's forefinger, they made their meandering way across the park to Portsmouth Square and the fireworks. All seven of them were given front-row chairs across from the Chinese Restaurant, the Pagoda Inn, on Jackson Street. This was where her mother and Captain Isaiah Lees had often met with the now-governor and then-mayor, Washington Bartlett to discuss the Chinatown murders of 1884.

They dined on a la carte bowls of chow mein, fried rice, and won ton. A tall Chinese gentleman named Wang Xiu Ying waited on them, and he kept their cups supplied with an interesting mint-flavored tea.

As the firework display began, she remembered her mother telling her that her former client, Andrew Kwong, of the Sam Yup Company, imported the variety of rockets and firecrackers directly from southern China. The concussion of explosions and the stream of sizzling colored lights across the sky, made everyone assembled gasp and proclaim in "oohs and ahs."

At one point, medicine man Hástin Yázhe rose from his chair and began to dance. He also chanted one of his songs, his arms and legs rising and falling like soft pistons, as he bellowed out a deep refrain to his gods. She watched, fascinated, as his head snapped back, and his dark face rose, taking in the explosive sky, as if these missiles had been sent directly to him from his ancient ancestors in China.

She watched Ajei bend over, and she thought she was going to rise and dance with her brethren. She did not. Instead, she began to wretch and vomit, falling over onto the grass, the spittle forming a ghastly puddle at her head. Her face was ashen, and she was at once agitated, her legs convulsing and her arms hugging her torso. After she and the medicine man tried to lift her, thinking she was ill from the meal, she began to sway, her eyes rolling back into her head, and she could not walk on her own.

"We must take her to the hospital at once," she told Hástin Yázhe. Together, with the others trailing behind, they grabbed onto the young woman's arms and began to drag her toward the nearest hansom carriage parked on Jackson Street. Just before they reached the carriage, a dark shadow passed before them. It ran across Jackson howling at the moon. It was a coyote.

Chapter 9: Criminal Trial, First Day

*San Francisco City Hall Courthouse, San Francisco, Wednesday,
July 6, 1887.*

Laura elbowed her way through the throng of demonstrators outside San Francisco City Hall. She could see the categories of sympathizers and protestors from the placards and signs they held up and the slogans they shouted. As usual, the suffragette contingent stood on soap boxes for these shorter female leaders to rise above the crowds, and their signs read: "Condemn the man who raped the child!" and, "Midwives support families and not the greedy hospitals!" The large majority of activists were against the defendant, and they were mostly white males. "Midwifery murders our unborn! Hospitals are for a healthy birth and pure motherhood!" Still others raved about Mrs. Fulbright's being Chinese and practicing medicine that was "pagan and dangerous witchcraft."

She visited Ajei in the hospital the day before; it was excruciatingly painful to see her ill. Ajei was nauseated and vomited frequently. The doctors said they did not know the cause of the young woman's malady, and this added to Laura's concern. Somehow, she believed their sexual relationship may have caused the sudden illness. The gossip columnist, Beatrice Holcombe, cast a light of fear over them both, and she speculated that one of their suspects may have decided to make Ajei the first victim. Now that she was going to argue her case, this possible threat was pressuring her even more. The articles about the trial the four women submitted to the newspapers were not yet published, not even in the *San Diego Bee* that Clara owned.

She never felt passionate love before. Ajei, with her inability to speak, was much more proficient with her physical communications. Dr. McFarland told her that he believed humans sang before they spoke. "How else would tribal societies develop oral traditions before written traditions? Why did the Navajo call their most potent spiritual medicine 'songs,' and how did the isolation of industrialization cause so many mentally ill victims?"

he said.

It was true. When they made love, Ajei sang. She may not speak words, but her brain sang beautifully rendered melodies. The young woman fashioned different tunes for each part of her lover's body, and Laura, her eyes shut, did not know whether her delicate touch would be on an arm, a leg, a breast, or even upon the most responsive treasures below her waist. During the most rapturous moments of their trysts, Ajei did something different each time, so Laura knew not what to expect, making the dalliance much more exciting and mysterious. A song for every part of her body.

The many years of ritual love-making with her former husband, Dr. Charles Gordon, his breath reeking of tobacco and liquor, his hands rough and forceful, made her see men as repulsive. After her divorce, the few times she sought the company of a gentleman in intimacy, she received much the same unimaginative treatment. Now that she had Ajei, and could possibly lose her, her pulse quickened, and her mind wandered. She needed to focus her organizational skills before she argued in front of the hard-won jury.

Judge Frederick Lattimore was a criminal courtroom referee who was quite fair. He had a big family, was a gentleman farmer with a large estate in Sausalito. When arguing before him, she sprinkled her arguments with agricultural metaphor and simile, and this pleased him. Her philosophy treated both judge and jury as if they were a garden. Each person was a separate crop, requiring different husbandry. Arguing for jury placement, the day before, she knew generally about the backgrounds of the twelve men, although each was presently only a number.

Unlike Clara, she approached the legal disputation using masculine logic. Men, for the most part, did not understand the social sphere. To them, all relations required a purpose and a specific goal. Acting from an emotional inspiration was seen as weak and without merit. Therefore, she always used a goal-oriented, *ipso-facto* approach. If you are an American citizen, you are required to behave according to its laws and regulations. Ignorance is no valid excuse. Facts were what determined reality.

She did not necessarily agree with this fact-based mentality, but it worked within the framework of a criminal trial, with male jurors and a male judge. Her opponent, District Attorney Edward B. Stonehill, was a man. In addition, he attempted to make a name for himself in the legal halls of San Francisco, and he performed his discovery judiciously.

On this first day, her rebuttals were prepared, and Mr. Stonehill supplied her with the State's evidence against her client as well as his list of witnesses. A late witness to cross-examine, in addition to the lead witness, Dr. Storer, was Dr. Liu Wei, Chief Acupuncturist, the only other person in the room when Penelope expired.

She made a point of never researching her opponent. To her, the argument at hand was what inspired her to rise to the occasion. The personality of the opposition, almost always a man, did not affect her strategy. She responded in the heat of the battle and to what he said and did inside the courtroom.

Judge Lattimore assigned the docket schedule for this trial for two days, even though the press and demonstrators could have lasted weeks covering anything they said. She prepared for her allotted time, most of which took place the next day. Judge Holmes testified then, when she presented her courtroom drama starring Navajo medicine man, Hástin Yázhe.

They had a brief rehearsal the day previously, at the Toy mansion, and she was pleased with how Trella Evelyn orchestrated the action and increased the drama. However, she knew when it came time for the prosecution's cross examination, the medicine man had to respond on his own. She coached him about what he could say. She also made certain he understood she would be there to protect him by giving hand signals when she believed he should not answer the question. She wished Ajei could be there to assist in the communications.

She was inside this courtroom many other times, but it was never this full. She noticed there were many suffragette supporters in the court who wore medical bandages over their mouths. This was a symbolic sign of women being silenced by men, especially as it concerned abortion. Most of her criminal trial cases took a few hours, at most, and they usually became finalized before a jury trial was ordered. If the defendant had no prior convictions, then the court usually put him or her on probation, with perhaps some public service required, depending upon the specific crime.

She defended against Clara Foltz in the Wheeler murder trial back in '81, and that gained quite a bit of attention in the press. The sex appeal of women confronting each another, their bosoms heaving; the handsome man, Mr. Wheeler, accused of killing his wife's sister, his lover, then cutting her up and stuffing her inside a suitcase. Clara should have won the case against Wheeler, but her younger co-counsel, a male assistant D. A., was aggravated playing second fiddle to a lead special counsel and a woman, so he presented some evidence that had not been supplied to the defense. However, she won the case upon appeal. Wheeler was later taken to trial again, by a different D. A., and he was finally convicted.

"Mrs. Fulbright, how are you this morning?"

She approached the left side of the bench where the Chinese midwife sat. Next to her was Ah Toy, who was there to translate any Chinese that Dr. Liu Wei might speak. She nodded at her assistant, and Ah Toy smiled.

She could see across the room that Mr. Stonehill lined his three witnesses for the day next to him like birds on one of those new telephone wires going up all around the city. She imagined their testimonies would also be transmitted inside those wires during, or shortly after, they were called to testify. She nodded politely at Stonehill, and he responded by loosening his red bowed necktie and frowning.

He was a "Fancy Dan," obviously outfitted to gain the jury's and the press's full attention. Silk black sack coat, white shirt with black-lined ruffles on the sleeves and collar, and mirror-shined dark Oxfords with white spats. His curly, long blonde hair was swept away and back from his forehead to serve as the proscenium to his ruddy-cheeked face.

Stonehill's aspect was an emotional marketplace. His eyebrows ready to furrow in concentration one moment, and rise in surprise the next, along with his full golden mustache. It all depended upon the topic and the person he was addressing.

The D. A. was about forty, she would imagine, and he had a baritone timbre in his voice. She expected he was a belligerent foe. He fit into the category of many men against whom she argued. They believed they won more respect by increasing the volume of their pronouncements. These men believed they frightened the fair sex into submission; but she proved, upon many an occasion, that sound logic was received with much more acuity.

After the bailiff introduced Judge Lattimore to the assembled, and Judge Lattimore instructed the jury and the chimney-smoking press corps in the gallery, Lattimore bade D. A. Fancy Pants to present his opening argument. She operated her opening statements the way she controlled her entire performance. She took notes.

Her success came because she remained flexible. Ready to spit poison and logic back at her opponent the way the exotic spitting cobras did in India. She knew the burden of proof was never hers, so she used lucidity as well as her holistic female brain's images to wrangle her way into the minds of the jurors. The constant mantra she repeated to herself during a trial, as defense attorney, was "reasonable doubt, reasonable doubt; you can get them off with reasonable doubt."

"Gentlemen of the jury, good day to you. I, as you know, represent the people of our entire society. Not just the men. Not just the women. Every person of legal age who can be adjudicated to be of sound mind must obey the criminal codes, established by the people's legal representatives to protect that outside society from harm by individuals who would disobey or break these codes. This has been so since that shining, blessed day when Moses came down the mountain with his tablets. Today, I am accomplishing a job that requires your special judgement."

Stonehill moved across the room from his podium to address each juror seated in the twelve-seat panel. He walked slowly down the four rows of three deep and stared at each man as he spoke.

"Without your intelligent and empathetic discernment of why this woman, this midwife, Mrs. Honora Fulbright, has broken the rules we have in place to protect our society, we might as well pack up our things and head home. Back to the farm, hotel, home, mansion, or boarding house. Without you, my fellow citizens, our people's jurors, the law does not function."

She jotted down that *he was attempting to gain favor by flattery*. She noticed that perhaps seven of them sat up straighter when he said "your special judgement," so she marked her juror chart with a special symbol in their little squares with their juror numbers inside the squares.

"I must prove beyond a reasonable doubt and with a preponderance of evidence that Mrs. Honora Fulbright over there is guilty of the extreme negligence required of the crime called involuntary manslaughter. Please be aware gentlemen. This is not a murder trial. There is no requirement to prove that this woman intended to kill Miss Penelope Farmer, the pregnant victim. It is my job to prove that she did not take the reasonable steps necessary to prevent what happened, which is gross negligence. That's why you shall hear from my expert witnesses. The first gentleman is a respected doctor in Mrs. Fulbright's own profession as an acupuncturist. In fact, he is her supervisor in Chinatown. Also, we have with us today the one man who can speak to the fact that any midwife practitioner is a danger to the lives of pregnant women— especially women who are too young to make an adult choice. I will establish what happened on the day in question, June 20, 1887, inside Mrs. Fulbright's home was an act of extreme negligence on the defendant's part. You will hear from the eyewitness, Dr. Liu Wei, and from the Medical Examiner, Dr. Hiram Philpot."

She noted that Stonehill did not refer to the fetus as a victim. Perhaps she could use Judge Holmes' testimony to pursue a different slant? How was the D. A. going to use the acupuncture expert? She believed she knew how Dr. Storer would be used. She spent a great deal of time researching trial transcripts of other abortion cases when he was called as a witness.

Stonehill had made his way to the end of the jury panel. He turned on his shiny heels and strutted back to the main podium near the bench. The members of the jury followed him with their eyes like baby hawks.

"If you pay attention, my fellow citizens, you will be able to come to the logical conclusion that this woman's actions were such that the death of Penelope Farmer was inevitable, under these special circumstances. I appreciate your time. May God assist us in our chosen duties."

She thought his opening was fairly straightforward. No tricks. No hints of deception. Actually, perhaps she could bring the deception to light. She knew enough not to grandstand the way she had with Trella Evelyn and Clara. The summation was when she did that. This was her chance to get these males' minds working toward the doubts she had to show them. Spraying a bit of poison never hurt anybody.

Judge Lattimore stared down at her. "Miss Gordon? How are you? Would you like to grace us with your opening statement?"

As she walked over to the podium, she was thinking *reasonable doubt and barnyard antics*. The images flowed into her mind's camera as she looked at the judge.

"Your honor. I am doing well. Were you able to stop Red? How many hens has he carried off? Five? Ten?"

The judge laughed. "A fox can chew through chicken wire, so I replaced it with weld mesh. I also don't use bone meal or blood, or fish and bone, in the chickens' feed. The smell attracts foxes. We haven't had one for a year now. Knock on wood."

She turned back to face her flock of roosters on the jury panel. "Gentleman. I second the emotion of our District Attorney. Without your judgement, our system has no way to function on behalf of the innocent accused. We have one of the few judicial systems in this world that protects the accused. Usually, it goes the other way. It's the defense attorney's job to prove his or her client's innocence. I believe we practice the best system because I protect my client's innocence."

She watched their faces. The men who had responded to Fancy Pants' reference to rules and responsibility were nodding their heads at her.

"On that note. I shall be showing you why Mrs. Fulbright

should remain innocent of these charges. Did you know Penelope Farmer, the sixteen-year-old victim, who was fifteen weeks pregnant when she pleaded for help from my client, had become pregnant by her own father?"

A few of the men cleared their throats. Still others showed a red flush on their necks and cheeks. She decided to continue spraying her poisonous venom a bit longer.

"Women in this society of ours are at a disadvantage, as I am certain you are all aware. You have wives. You have paramours. You have relatives who are female. Even though we women cannot sit where you are today, even though my client is supposedly guaranteed a trial by a jury of her peers, she is not afraid of what you will do. Why is that? It seems our law allows that confessions made on a deathbed are admissible evidence of the truth. Truth. What a noble concept. Did you know that the ancient definition of truth by the Greeks was *Aletheia*, which meant 'unclosedness', 'unconcealedness', 'disclosure,' and, literally, 'the state of not being hidden'?"

She noticed that they were now looking at her with quizzical stares. That was good. That was, in fact, her purpose.

"Most uneducated people believe the truth is a fact or the correctness and belief that something has occurred which can be traced to a single unalterable source or cause. Not so. It is a much more complicated concept, as I will be demonstrating throughout this trial. I know you intelligent men understand this. My task, if you will, is to uncover and reveal to you very logical alternative explanations for you to compare with what my honorable opponent will be suggesting was the real truth behind what took place on June 20th inside my client's place of employment. If you agree with my alternatives to the point where they outweigh the very linear and solid explanations Mr. Stonehill gives you, then you must acquit Mrs. Fulbright of these charges being made against her."

She saw them nodding. Her doubtful seed was planted.

"Your doubt only need rise to a level of reasonableness but not certainty. Would a reasonable person, and I am very certain you are all most reasonable gentlemen, believe that my alternative propositions reveal a more logical explanation or cause? Not the usual meaning of being true. Just so that your minds think I've uncovered reasonable doubt, which tips the scales of justice slightly in her favor. Then you must acquit. Thank you."

She did not stare. She did not brow beat. She merely explained how they must use their brains to be fair to her client, who was innocent until proven guilty. No objections. She baffled these men once more. She was ready to play.

"Mr. Stonehill. You may call your first witness," Judge Lattimore barked.

She listened carefully to the testimonies of both the Medical Examiner, Mr. Philpot, and the acupuncture supervisor, Dr. Liu Wei. Stonehill asked the usual technical questions to establish the conditions under which the victim had been subjected before she died. She countered Philpot's sworn statement that the girl had died because of "miscarriage caused by blood loss from induced pressure," by asking him the specific question of where the fetus was during this miscarriage. She knew he must answer that Penelope Farmer's pregnancy was "ectopic," so he ultimately responded that the fetus was improperly growing on the victim's left ovary, which could have caused the stomach pain, dizziness, and bleeding from the miscarriage event under Mrs. Fulbright's care.

However, when Dr. Liu Wei was called to the stand, Stonehill had an ace up his sleeve. He asked Judge Lattimore if he could demonstrate to the court how the procedure the defendant performed on the victim could have caused contractions on a pregnant female of fifteen weeks. She objected that the fact that her client had an ectopic pregnancy made her condition quite different than a normal pregnancy, and her client was unaware of her patient's condition. Thus, such a demonstration would not be equivalent.

Stonehill, on the other hand, pointed out that it did not matter what type of pregnancy Penelope had, since it was the responsibility of the midwife to know about her patient's condition in the first place. Also, if this specific acupuncturist procedure indeed can cause a miscarriage, then Mrs. Fulbright's negligence would make her responsible for the resulting death of the mother. The D. A. was still not mentioning the death of the fetus, so she assumed he was not going to discuss its role in the procedure.

The judge ruled in the prosecutor's favor, and what Dr. Liu Wei presented was a "circus act" that would perhaps rival her own presentation of the "doctor of tribal medicine," Hástin Yázhe, which would occur tomorrow. The pregnant Chinese woman the acupuncturist brought up to the special demonstration area in front of the judge's bench was, it was announced, fifteen weeks and two days pregnant. Although she was not ectopically pregnant, she was approximately the same age, height, and weight as the deceased, Penelope Farmer.

The doctor began to perform the same procedure that was demonstrated on her by her client, Mrs. Fulbright. All three points were pressed on the woman's body: *Sanyinjiao*, *Zhiyin*, and *Hegu*. After ten minutes following the doctor's pressure applications, the young woman began to groan, then she clutched her stomach with both hands, and she began to writhe in her chair at the table. Her screams were in Cantonese. Ah Toy leaned over and whispered, "She damns the doctor to *Diyu*. Hell." She imagined that was quite appropriate, and she wondered who had written their script.

"She now contracts. She will miscarriage prematurely," the doctor told the court. She noticed the jury members. All but two had transfixed their stares upon the woman as if she were performing some kind of voodoo contortion. During jury selection, she uncovered the fact that only two of the men had ever witnessed a woman giving birth, and they were the husbands.

The doctor moved back to his chair and grabbed the woman's leg in his hands. He grasped her ankle and pressured *Sanyinjiao*, and she immediately stopped having her alleged premature contractions. She had a difficult time believing Stonehill would attempt such an obvious ruse.

She rose from her seat. "Your honor, I believe the rooster wants us to believe the Chinese kite that he's flying over the hen house is a hawk. Without a medical doctor's verification of the kind lady's alleged contractions, how are we to have complete agreement that she indeed has experienced them?"

Several members of the gallery laughed. She could see her barnyard analogy had brought a smile to Lattimore's face. Mr. Stonehill continued his interview of Dr. Liu Wei, establishing the time of the procedure her client administered upon Penelope Farmer and whether she had examined the girl before she performed the acupuncture.

She knew she had to rebut this testimony, so she asked the doctor if Miss Farmer's condition was an emergency. He said the girl had called Mrs. Fulbright's clinic and told her that she had missed twice, and she asked if Mrs. Fulbright had pills or procedures to bring her around. She answered Miss Farmer in the affirmative, and the appointment was made for later that same afternoon.

"The Medical Examiner's report and testimony said Miss Farmer had heroin in her blood. Did Mrs. Fulbright administer this to her?" She wanted the doctor to establish this fact for the jury.

"Yes, the girl had complained of extreme pain, so it was administered in pill form before the procedure took place," he responded.

"Let me get these facts straight. Mrs. Fulbright was acting upon an emergency. She was not going to treat the patient with the usual surgery administered by physicians to extract the fetus to remove it quickly. No, she treated Miss Farmer's agonizing pain, and she never, at any time, entered the young woman's uterus. Is that correct?"

Stonehill objected. He said that treating the woman with a dangerous drug such as heroin was also reckless and dangerous to the life of the girl and her child.

"Again, your honor. Mrs. Fulbright did not know about the ectopic pregnancy of Penelope Farmer. She administered the pain killer because it is sold as a patent medicine, and it is not deemed dangerous by the government," she countered.

Judge Lattimore took some time to think. "Although I agree with you that heroin is not deemed dangerous, under the current laws of California, yet I have personally seen victims in my court who have become slaves to the parent drug, opium, and heroin, opium's child, to my mind, is *quite* dangerous. However, since the technicality of the law is at stake here, I must overrule your objection, Mr. Prosecutor."

She knew that was a minor victory, so she restated it for the jury. "Mrs. Honora Fulbright was acting in the best interests of her patient, and she was not endangering the young woman's life by administering the heroin tablets."

There was a commotion in the gallery. Judge Lattimore had to clear his court of two men. One man was shouting about the Chinese and how they made millions of dollars on opium by "addicting us and selling it in their Chinatown dens." He also screamed that their drugs caused wars that killed hundreds of thousands of people. The second man actually ran toward Mrs. Fulbright as if to harm her. Two officers needed to restrain him and drag him bodily outside and to jail.

The judge called for a lunch recess, and she spent her time down the street at the public hospital with Ajei. Her lover was recovering, drinking liquids and keeping them down, and she shared a chicken breast sandwich with her. The attending physician, a Dr. Hodges, said that the Navajo woman's illness was most likely caused by the change in her diet. She promised Ajei she would return after the day's trial session.

Back in court, she knew that morning's histrionics were just the preliminary sideshow to the main event of the afternoon. She watched the prosecution's table, as Dr. Horatio Storer prepared his notes and adjusted his tie. He also combed his beard, of all things, as if the unkempt appearance of a few stray gray hairs might reflect upon his expertise. She knew he had recovered from tuberculin infection and had returned to the States to testify for this trial.

"Mr. Prosecutor. Call your final witness," Judge Lattimore shouted over the din. "Silence! Or, I shall have you all expelled from my courtroom!"

Whatever the judge had for lunch had obviously not agreed with him. She imagined a row of trumpeters on either side of Storer, heralding his appearance, as he marched to the witness stand. If the Scarlet Sisters could do it then why not him?

After the doctor was sworn in, Mr. Stonehill approached

him. "Dr. Storer, we are very honored to have you sail from Europe to be with us. Your reputation as an expert gynecologist and member of the American Medical Association, as well as someone who has testified in many other cases of this ilk around the country, has made you a respected representative for women's health care. Could you please tell the court why you believe the occupation of midwife is not safe for our women?"

She could not object to that, as he was, most certainly, a recognized expert, so she just listened. She was, in fact, beginning to worry about matching this doctor with her own witch doctor the next day.

"I have nothing, per se, against the occupation. I simply protest the fact that these women work at home, under non-sterile conditions. And some, in a most dangerous practice, use surgical tools to ply their trade. To my mind, these women need to work inside a hospital where their activities can be monitored by doctors, just the way nurses are in the hospitals we in the A.M.A. have approved. They should never be allowed to perform murder on a living child in the womb."

Stonehill nodded. "In this instance, do you believe Mrs. Fulbright, even though she was a member of the Women's Obstetrics Society, was performing an unsafe or inherently dangerous procedure on her patient, Penelope Farmer?"

She stood up. "I object, your honor. As we have seen, just moments before, the acupuncture procedure was not proved beyond a doubt to be inherently dangerous to the woman. No objective medical doctor verified that it indeed caused the contractions. The Medical Examiner stated it was, most likely, the ectopic pregnancy which caused the hemorrhaging. In fact, we don't know if this substitute woman was playing a role, as if she were having a miscarriage in order to help the prosecutor prove a point."

The judge stared at Stonehill, then at Dr. Storer. "Gentlemen? Do you believe it was the procedure itself that caused the reckless negligence? I need clarification from this witness on that point, and I'm certain the jury does as well."

Some male member in the audience yelled out, "She's a

charlatan and a pagan! She should not practice her witchcraft on women!"

Lattimore struck his gavel down hard on the wooden block. "Silence! One more outburst, and I'll have this court cleared of any spectators! Dr. Storer, would you please continue?"

The witness looked over at Mrs. Fulbright seated next to her at the defense table. "Thank you, judge. I have spent some time questioning this woman, and researching her profession and the way she practices it. Although she is very knowledgeable of the female anatomy and especially its processes after the miracle of gestation has occurred, she is not aware that any interruption during these biological stages may cause a dangerous physical or mental reaction in the pregnant female. As a result of this ignorance, she did not, in this instance, stop to examine the uterus before she began her Chinese medical procedure. This, in and of itself, in my considered opinion, is negligence, per se. If she had examined the patient before she began, she would have been mandated to call in a surgeon who could have addressed the ectopic presence of the infant growing on her left ovary, perhaps saving her life."

She wanted to object, but she was afraid Stonehill had gone down this path on purpose. Instead, she had another idea in mind, and she would bring it out during her cross examination.

"Very well. Thank you, Dr. Storer. I shall overrule the objection by defense counsel," Judge Lattimore said. "You may continue, Mr. Stonehill."

"I have no further questions, your honor," Stonehill said.

"Very well. Miss Gordon? You may question the witness," Lattimore nodded at her.

She took a sheet of paper with her as she approached the witness. This would take some amount of sly inuendo, and she was prepared.

"Dr. Storer. We are indeed very honored to have you in court today to testify as an expert on these matters. In point of fact, did you not begin the campaign in the 1860s to have legislation passed in all the states and territories to make all surgeries to remove a fetus, even before quickening, a criminal offense, except in the rare instances when the mother's life was in imminent danger? And, in addition, that these so-called emergency surgeries to save the mother must be done by doctors who are members of the American Medical Association?"

The doctor smiled and nodded. "Yes, I am proud to say, our efforts to save the lives of our future generations have proven successful, for the most part. There is still much more work to be done to educate the public concerning safety, such as in this case, but we believe humanity is better off in the long run."

She returned the smile and looked down at her paper. "I first learned about these emergency abortions through my reading of this passage from the *Textbook of Obstetrics and Gynaecology*, published mid-century, which reveals that these abortions were accomplished with a variety of specialized perforating and forceps-like instruments, which include cranioclasts, trepans, and basiotribes. Are these the instruments used most often?"

"Yes, that text is approved by the A.M.A., and we do authorize the instruments of which you speak. Of course, the procedure is to save the mother's life in late pregnancy, in extreme emergencies after quickening," Dr. Storer pointed out.

"And, is the basic purpose of these emergency surgeries to reduce the cranial circumference of the infant in order to quickly remove the fetal body with the least possible trauma to the woman's body?"

"Yes. The life of the mother is at grave risk, and we must act quickly," Storer responded.

"I have read the statistics on these procedures, doctor. Isn't it a fact that in over eighty percent of the time, the infant is killed by using this procedure?"

"I object! This line of inquiry is not relevant nor is it material to the charges against the defendant," Stonehill shouted.

She knew this would happen. She simply wanted to set up the witness for her final *coup de grace*.

"I retract my statement, your honor. I want to ask one final question of the good doctor. Since you are also a surgeon, you must have performed many procedures on women, have you not?" She wanted his full attention, and she knew asking him about his profession was the best way to get it.

"Of course. In fact, my methods have been written up in many medical journals and school manuals around the world."

"Excellent. Therefore, in this case, since you disprove of my client's actions treating Penelope Farmer's ectopic pregnancy, what would you have done if she had come to you in her panicked and hysterical state of mind and physical emergency?"

She was hoping for the right response, but she could not be certain he would give it. She was playing upon his ego, the only card she had left.

"This is a very obvious case. I have treated women like this hundreds of times in my career. They are mentally unsound, and the only certain process to cure a mentally hysterical young woman is to remove the ovaries—both of them. The ovariotomy is the most common operation for such maladies. For women like Miss Farmer, who have become habitually thievish, profane, or obscene, despondent or self-indulgent, shrewish or fatuous, the best solution is to remove the cause of their mental illness: the reproductive organs."

She saw that many of the women in the gallery who were wearing the medical patches over their mouths, ripped them off, and shouted their protests.

She waited until there was silence again following the judge's gavel strikes.

"That is quite interesting, Dr. Storer. I would imagine then, all things being considered fair and equal, you would treat a whoring, lying, and raving maniac, who happened to be a man, in the same manner, would you not?" She smiled at him, but he was, quite obviously, confused.

"I don't understand what you mean. Could you clarify that question?"

She noticed there was perspiration on his brow. She turned toward the jury panel.

"I mean, Dr. Storer, would you remove these insane men's testicles to cure them?"

As she walked away from the witness stand, a widening grin was spreading across her face. The judge was banging his gavel, the gallery was in an uproar, and she turned to look at the faces of the twelve jurors. Every one of them, each and every man, had the expression she had only previously seen on the countenances of the swine boars she had castrated back on the farm in Pennsylvania.

Chapter 10: Criminal Trial, Second Day

San Francisco City Hall Courthouse, San Francisco, Wednesday, July 7, 1887.

Laura spent the previous night at the hospital, and she fell asleep, lying on the bed, holding Ajei's hand. She knew she needed to assuage her brain after the emotional turmoil that was day one of the trial. This new day was her final opportunity to turn the tables on the prosecution and its misogynist witness, Dr. Horatio Storer. She would never change the national opinion against a woman's right to terminate an unwanted pregnancy, but if she could show the ineptitude of the present law, perhaps the future members of society would think more carefully about the entire problem until women obtained the right to vote.

On July 5, when she met with Trella Evelyn, Clara, and the Scarlet Sisters, to plan and rehearse the dramatic testimony of the tribal medicine man, Hástin Yázhe, they decided it would be more advantageous to have the Navajo enter the courtroom just before testifying. He was going to wear his complete regalia, and the visual response by the jury would be accelerated from the experience of viewing him.

Inside the courtroom, as she walked down the center aisle, she saw there were even more people in the gallery. The same suffragettes had their mouths taped shut, and the men were puffing like steam engines on a variety of pipes, cigars and cigarettes. The numbers of photographers up in the balcony had increased so much that many of them were pushed against the front railings. Precariously, they jostled with other men for a better angle on the proceedings going on below. The tension was thick in the air. These people expected to see a carnival side show, but it was her purpose to present an alternative to her client's alleged negligence in the case of the death of Penelope Farmer.

At the defense table, three of her witnesses were present. Mrs. Althea Crutchfield, Penelope's tutor, and the distinguished judge, and Massachusetts Supreme Court Justice, Oliver Wendell

Holmes, Junior. She greeted them both, and they smiled up at her. The third witness was Dr. Andrew McFarland, who was also going to testify at Clara's civil trial the next day. She knew the doctor from earlier cases, and he was going to testify about the mental state of Penelope when she visited Mrs. Fulbright's clinic.

Judge Holmes wore an old-fashioned blue frock coat with fur on the lapels, a rounded collar, and a bowed tie the color of blood. His penetrating blue eyes held the wisdom of his years on the bench, and his light-brown handlebar mustache framed a strong chin. At age forty-six, he looked much younger, as he had a thin countenance and ruddy cheeks. She knew how she wanted to question him. His father had been a medical doctor, and Oliver junior had served in the Civil War and was wounded. Like the prosecution's key witness, Dr. Storer, Holmes was a distinguished Harvard alum, but he knew the law as it applied in this case, especially the prosecution's allegations of criminal negligence. Judge Holmes was to be her second witness of the day.

After interviewing Mr. Farmer's household staff, what she was presenting today did not seem as far-fetched. Mrs. Althea Crutchfield, in fact, was her first witness. She provided the jury with the chronological details concerning the victim's "True Woman" education to become civilized. She then compared this accepted teaching method with the girl's tribal education, and how Penelope, with the help of her mother, Haseya, and the medicine man, was eventually transformed into believing she was a witch and skinwalker.

"*Yee naaldooshii* means skinwalkers, as the medicine man explained to me. Skinwalkers are holy people who can change into an animal to protect the sacred ancestral traditions," Mrs. Crutchfield explained, and Laura could see the jurors were attentive upon her every word.

She continued to question the teacher about what she learned about the Navajo's tribal ways and how the medicine man told the two Farmer women, as ancestral witches, that they were obligated to protect their people. When the jury heard the conservative and educated tutor relate the vivid details about witnessing the girl transform, following Haseya's death, into her mother's exact appearance, she saw them lean forward in their chairs in rapt attention.

"She began to wear her mother's clothing. I saw her face and mannerisms transform into the exact duplicate of Haseya Farmer. She slept in her mother's bedroom, and she did all the chores, giving orders to the staff the way her mother did before she died. And then, in the shadows of early twilight, on the night before she visited Mrs. Fulbright, I saw the girl's face momentarily transmute into the trembling snout, the flashing teeth, and the yipping yowl of a coyote."

Of course, the prosecutor contradicted the tutor's testimony with questions about her mental health. Mrs. Crutchfield had been under the care of an alienist for her nightmares following the experience she had at the Farmer mansion.

Laura countered his inquisition with the fact Mrs. Crutchfield saw the alienist following her tribulations as a tutor and that her psychological stability was quite good before that event took place. Stonehill also asked Mrs. Crutchfield if she believed Penelope actually changed into another human being or animal, and she admitted to him that "her empirical senses" did not understand what was happening.

These responses were important to the next question she wanted to ask. It was an underlying key to understanding Penelope and her mental state that day.

"When Miss Farmer was wearing her mother's clothing, did you see her father, Aloysius, enter her bedroom at night?"

Stonehill fumed, "I object, your honor! How does this inquiry relate to Mrs. Fulbright's criminal negligence?"

Judge Lattimore stared at her. "Well, counselor? Can you explain yourself?"

"Judge, if you will approve my inquiry, I am attempting to prove a direct sequence of events which leads to a defense of the alleged negligent act at Mrs. Fulbright's clinic. In point of fact, I shall follow up Mrs. Crutchfield's testimony with my three other witnesses. This present answer will be added to my locomotive of logical progression, as one adds boxcars filled with cargo headed to a pre-determined destination. My destination is just over the horizon, your honor, I promise you."

"Very well. I shall hold you to that promise, Miss Gordon. Objection overruled. You may answer the question, Mrs. Crutchfield," Lattimore said.

"Yes, I did see Mr. Farmer enter the bedroom upon three occasions when I was working late," Mrs. Crutchfield responded, looking down at her lap.

"Thank you, Mrs. Crutchfield, you may step down."

She turned to the jury as her witness walked back to the defense table.

"I would like the court to reflect again on the fact that Penelope Farmer, seconds before she expired at the clinic, named Mr. Aloysius Farmer as the father of her child."

The gallery erupted in shouts of "Whore," "Fraud," and "Rapist." Judge Lattimore pounded on his gavel block. When the crowd subsided, he said, "Call your next witness."

"I call Judge Oliver Wendall Holmes, Junior to the stand, your honor," she said.

The magnesium ribbon flashes from the balcony ignited, and the photographs of the great legal luminary were affixed to the cameras' dry plates for the evening editions of newspapers. Judge Holmes was sworn in, he climbed into the witness chair, and she approached him. Her heart was racing, simply from the nervousness she was feeling to be interrogating such a famous legal scholar.

"Thank you so very much for traveling out to California to be with us. Mr. Holmes, are you not at present a sitting Supreme Court Judge in the State of Massachusetts?"

He smiled. "I am not, at present, a sitting judge. At present, I am a sitting witness who is masquerading as a judge."

There was a scattering of laughter.

"Very well, but I am interested in your experience as an adjudicator and legal theorist, whose opinions have been referenced by many barristers around the world. In point of fact, I am especially interested in your writings in a book you wrote in 1881 entitled *The*

Common Law. More specifically, I would like you to lend your expertise concerning the legal concept of criminal negligence. Most importantly, as it relates to this case, could you explain your understanding of how negligence can be objectively found as opposed to the subjective fault method?"

Judge Holmes cleared his throat and spoke as if he were lecturing to beginning law students. She realized that compared to his experience on the bench in New England, San Francisco and California jurisprudence must seem to be a frontier outpost.

"Thank you, Miss Gordon. I am pleased you did not ask me to apply my knowledge to the facts in this case. This has been requested of me in the past by attorneys who, I suppose, were hoping beyond hope that I could do their work for them."

Again, there was laughter in the courtroom.

"The life of the common law has not been logic. The life of the law is based on experience. My experience with the common law is in this book. I wrote it because I believe it is the legal professional's job to argue a specific case using the unique facts at hand. And, in a jury trial, the opposing attorneys' jobs are to explain to the defendant's peers, the civilian citizens on that jury, how each barrister sees these facts as they relate to the charges being made against the innocent defendant. The judge, you see, is merely a person who can get the arguers back on track. As you were referencing a locomotive earlier, I would hitch a ride and say that the judge is the conductor and not the engineer. The engineer, in my mind, is the jury driving the legal train of thought to its destination. Let's just call that destination justice, for want of a better word."

She saw that the members of the jury were nodding in agreement. Judge Lattimore also nodded when Holmes referenced him in his use of metaphor. District Attorney Stonehill was rather stone-faced.

"The law does not see us as God sees us. When God sees us, it is through a personal and moral lens. When the law sees us, it is through an institutional lens which focuses upon serving the welfare of society. If a person is born hasty or awkward, he or she cannot claim this birth defect as an excuse for breaking the law. Being prone to accidents is recognized in the courts of heaven, but not in the courts of this life. Why? Because congenital slips are just as troublesome to a neighbor as if they sprang from guilty neglect."

She nodded. "You do not mean, of course, that there are never any excuses that can be made. Certainly, if a person were insane or younger than an adult, the law would make an exception, correct?"

"The exceptions you speak of are to be applied by each case's requirements. I speak of a need for the law to have an objective standard by which to assess each case. The law considers what would be blameworthy in the person of ordinary intelligence and prudence, and determines liability by that. Being accident prone, even because of a birth defect such as blindness, does not exclude one from possible guilt. Why? Because if the judge or jury determines this person was of sound mind, then he is required to foresee the possible dangers he can cause from his blindness. Of course, if the blind person were also of unsound mind or was a young child, then a reasonable person would not believe this person to be guilty of a negligent act."

She realized he was speaking of the law's need for an objective way to determine negligence. "Can you give the court an example from your experience deciding such cases? Perhaps one that incorporates this reasonable person theory?"

"Yes, I can. In fact, I have always begun my thinking with the understanding that the appreciation of intent is not limited to humans. A dog, who is tripped over, realizes the difference between this accident and the intentional kick he might receive from an angry human's foot. This is why we must attempt to minimize intent in cases of negligence, even though it cannot be ignored completely. That is because inside the actor's human brain, the infinite variety of possible intentions becomes almost impossible to verify objectively. My case concerned that of a Dr. Pierce. This good doctor, who, by all other considerations, seemed to be of good moral standing and professional integrity and intelligence, was accused of gross negligence when treating a patient's wounds by applying kerosene-soaked rags to her skin. Even though his intent was not voiced, he was accused of murder and convicted. I agreed with said conviction. Why? It was not clear from the facts in Pierce whether the defendant had simply been oblivious to the danger of using kerosene-soaked rags or whether he had made the wrong cost versus benefit judgment about whether the danger outweighed the potential benefit. In the pure case of not knowing of the danger, the fault lies in Dr. Pierce's having failed to investigate the risks attendant upon his affirmative conduct of treating the patient."

"I see. The objective standard of the law requiring a person of reasonable intelligence to have known the inherent danger of applying kerosene to wounds replaces the required intent necessary to prove murder. Pierce's intent was implied by his gross neglect, is that correct?"

Holmes nodded back at her. "Correct. Pierce is liable for his act of omission. The only field of law that is structured in the same way as the standard analysis of negligence in torts is liability for omissions--both in torts and criminal law. However, no one is liable for an omission unless there is a duty to intervene and prevent the harm from occurring. Pierce is guilty of murder because of this duty of his as a doctor to prevent the harm of his patient."

"Therefore, you are saying that because of Pierce's duty to act, he was responsible for the murder of his patient, despite the absence of malice or an intent to do harm?" She was cornering the judge for her grand purposes.

"Yes. By the standard that I placed upon him by society's general expectations of doctors in his profession and how they must act in the best welfare interests of that society."

She nodded. "Of course, if we have no malicious intent necessary to be proved, as in the case of criminal involuntary manslaughter, then the act itself must be heinous enough that a medical professional's duty was then breached. In addition, I would assume, the victim of such a negligent act must also be aware that the medical professional's usual practice is inherently dangerous, also, no?"

Judge Holmes chuckled. "I see where you are headed with your locomotive, Miss Gordon. My Dr. Pierce was a general practitioner. Therefore, the dangers inherent in his work were minimal. Thus, when he applied the kerosene-soaked rags to his patient's wounds, his act seemed grossly negligent under the common rules of his job. In your example, if the medical practitioner's job is inherently dangerous, such as that of surgeon, for example, then it would be necessary for the patient to be aware of this and to agree to the treatment, preferably by signing a document which assessed the possible risks of that surgery."

"I object, your honor! Despite Judge Holmes' admonition that he would not argue the defense's case for her, he is doing just that. In addition, this child was a minor, and there was no legally binding waiver signed by an adult." Stonehill's face was red and his arms were flailing about like a rooster's wings with his head severed.

"Judge Lattimore, sir, if you please. My client's general practice is not surgery. It is acupuncture. In addition, since the only living parent who could sign for the victim was also the father of her child, Mrs. Fulbright could not, in good conscience, provide the legal waiver. As I shall prove, my client's patient was under extreme psychological and physical duress. Time was of the essence in this emergency. Indeed, most of the causes of this duress were unknown to Mrs. Fulbright. Her duty of care was to a young woman who was pregnant because of special circumstances, which became known only at the last moment of her life on this Earth."

Judge Lattimore frowned down at her. "Your locomotive is now passing my farm, Miss Gordon. If you want me to ride, then you must explain where you're going with these new thoughts of yours. Your client is accused of gross negligence leading to the death of Penelope Farmer. Are you heading in the proper direction?"

"Yes, I believe I am, your honor. My next witness, Dr. Andrew McFarland, in fact, will supply another boxcar to this train of thought. May I call him to continue? My train stops at all farms along the way," she said, smiling.

"Do you have any questions of this witness?" Judge Lattimore looked over at Mr. Stonehill.

"No, your honor," the prosecutor said, between gritted teeth.

"Very well. You may continue. The witness may step down," Judge Lattimore instructed.

She was pleased with herself when she saw Judge Holmes wink at her as he passed by. Dr. McFarland knew exactly what she was going to ask, as she had coached him the day before.

"Dr. McFarland, you are an alienist and physician, are you not? Also, you have testified as an expert witness in many legal trials around the United States, is that not also true?"

Dr. McFarland raised his bushy, auburn eyebrows. "True on both accounts, Miss Gordon," he replied.

"The specific area of your expertise about which I want to ask is your knowledge of the Navajo tribal ways and religious beliefs. You have done some research on your recent trip to Arizona territory, is that correct?"

"Yes, and I have also been doing my own research concerning most of the tribes in this great land of ours," he said.

"Did you discuss with Navajo medicine man, Hástin Yázhe, about what occurred in the Farmer household before Miss Penelope Farmer became pregnant? Before the young woman sought the emergency help from my client, the midwife, Mrs. Honora Fulbright, and after Penelope's mother, Haseya, had died?"

Dr. McFarland nodded. "Yes. I questioned him thoroughly."

She walked over to the jury panel. "Dr. McFarland, in your capacity as a medical doctor and alienist, who is familiar with the Navajo tribal customs, can you give the court your considered opinion about what the mental state of Penelope Farmer was leading up to her death inside Mrs. Fulbright's clinic on June 20, 1887?"

"Objection, your honor. What does the mental state of the victim have to do with the defendant's gross negligence?"

"Your honor, I beg your patience once more. This train to justice needs another boxcar. Dr. McFarland and my final witness, Mr. Hástin Yázhe, will be establishing the fact that on the day of the alleged negligent act Penelope Farmer was under the extreme delusion that she was a tribal skinwalker or witch, who was doing the bidding of the tribal medicine man. My client had no way of knowing her patient was deranged and could not determine her

125

mental state. Nor, according to our previous esteemed legal scholar, Judge Holmes, was my client performing an act that rose to the extremes which make it life-threatening. In fact, your honor, I want to show that it was Penelope Farmer's mental state which led to her own death, not the actions of my client."

She held her breath. If Judge Lattimore didn't allow her to continue, her entire train could derail before it could arrive at the depot.

Judge Lattimore stared down at her, and then he glanced over at Mr. Stonehill. "Mr. District Attorney, I understand your incredulity. I am also inclined to agree that what Miss Gordon is attempting to prove is out of bounds. However, we have a unique dilemma here. If Miss Farmer can be shown to believe in her native religion, and her extreme position as a tribal witch, then her mental state at the time of her treatment by the defendant could be seen as quite stressful to her. I want to hear from Dr. McFarland about how this kind of internal stress can affect a person's physical well being. Therefore, I'll overrule your objection at this juncture." He turned back to look down at her. "You may continue, Miss Gordon."

"Thank you, your honor. Again, Dr. McFarland. Could you explain what you learned after your interview with the Navajo tribal medicine man?"

"Yes, but I believe it would be best to give some background as to the history of the Navajo and their culture as it compares with our own. We were, after all, the ones who defeated most of the native tribes all over the United States. The Navajo, or Holy People, should be given consideration, even though their culture was mostly an oral one rather than a written one."

She nodded. "I agree. How would you assess the Navajo culture's importance leading up to this time in history?"

"I believe it interesting to note that the Navajo, even in their tribal stories, or songs, have always allowed for others to be an acceptable part of their existence. Whereas our culture, for example, saw most tribes as a hindrance on our way to our Manifest Destiny and progress, the Navajo tended to adapt to others, including the Spanish, the Mexicans, other tribes in the area, and to us. They even created origin myths to explain where these others came from and how they should be treated. Even after their return from the harsh conditions at the forced migration to the Bosque Redondo, the Navajo did not believe they were victims. They assumed an active role in their own future and were vigorously involved in the expansion of their frontiers, such as they were. The Navajos adapted their strategies to the conditions of their foes. Until today, the twin strategies of defense short of war and an ethnocentric belief in their culture has kept them at peace with North Americans."

She looked over at the jury members. "What role did their religion play in this adaptive strategy? My next witness, for example, was educated in England. At Oxford, as a matter of fact. And yet, he decided he could help his people better by returning to the territories."

"Their religion is fairly adaptive as well, especially as it concerns nature and nature's requirements for their personal well being. Whereas our Bible stresses the conquest of our environment for our personal gain, their religious beliefs stress adapting to that environment because it gives them life. They believe they do not come from a heaven in the clouds but from the earth, several levels deep, beneath their feet. Whereas our Hades is below, their primal source is below. All of the strangers, or aliens, who appear around them, therefore, are also given origin stories related to these natural surroundings. However, whenever they are threatened in a personal way, this religion can become vindictive, just as our own Christian religion was against non-believers—most especially the Jews—during the Inquisition years. And, the way the European Reformation was against the Catholics."

"What exactly *did* happen when Mr. Aloysius Farmer took Haseya for his bride? Did she lose her status in the tribe? Did she become an American?" She wanted to bring her witness around to the subject at hand.

"Haseya was always considered by her tribe to be a witch or what they term a skinwalker, the *yee naaldooshii*. Therefore, when she moved with her new husband off the reservation and into San Francisco's high society, she had not given up her ways. She did not

127

learn English, and yet she did adapt, in the way of her people, in order to best serve her husband's new culture."

"And, what was the turning point which drove her back to her primitive beliefs?" She walked along the jury panel rows, looking at each member.

"According to the medicine man, who was called in to treat her, it was her consumption, which she contracted following a trip back to the reservation with her husband and daughter. She informed him and her daughter that her husband, in fact, had changed."

"Changed? In what manner had he changed?" She was getting close to the nexus of her argument.

"On the night after she was diagnosed by the American physician to have contracted consumption, Haseya had a dream. She predicted that her husband would change for the worse. And that dream came true. He was, one week later, seen beating her and cursing at her. On her death bed, in fact, the mother told her daughter that she was also a witch."

She walked to the end of the row and turned back around to face Dr. McFarland. "How, according to what you learned, was this to transpire? Were these two women, these two skinwalkers, obligated to do anything for the tribe?"

"Yes, according to tradition, they must exact revenge upon those who mistreat the Diné, or Holy People, the Navajo. In point of fact, and you may verify this with the next witness, they must kill two persons for each witch who dies. That means, strangely enough, that they can pursue their enemies even after death."

There were gasps from the gallery.

"And these skinwalker witches take which form to accomplish this retribution?"

"They can take any form, but usually they are in an animal's body, such as a coyote or a crow."

"In your considered opinion, Dr. McFarland, do you believe that Penelope Farmer, who was under the stress of her tribal spiritual obligations, and was being raped by her own father, could have become mentally ill to the point of physical danger?"

She had reached her point of no return. The jury was

impressed. The gallery was enthralled. This was Dr. McFarland's moment. He repeated what he had earlier told their discovery group at the Toy mansion.

"In my practice, and in the asylum statistics I have perused over the years, over twenty percent of deaths were said to be caused from stress exhaustion. When I examined the specifics of these cases, I discovered that the patients were suffering from delusional anxieties and manias which caused the stress leading directly to the breakdown of the body's vital organs. I believe Miss Penelope Farmer could very well have reached a stress point whereby her physical health was in extreme danger of collapse."

At that moment, a nurse burst through the courtroom's wide entry doors. She rushed up to the defense table and approached Laura. The nurse reached out to cup her right hand around her ear.

"Miss Gordon. Our patient, Miss Ajei, has been arrested. She was inside the maternity ward while a new mother was breastfeeding her infant. She was seen by the attending nurse to give this mother a cup of tea. About an hour following, both the mother and the infant began to wretch and vomit profusely. They have died, Miss Gordon. And the tea from which the young mother drank is suspected to be poisoned."

Chapter 11: Hunt

San Francisco City Hall Courthouse, San Francisco, Wednesday, July 7, 1887.

After she heard the news about Ajei being arrested at the public hospital, Laura realized she was putting another Navajo in jeopardy by having him testify. He was now coming through the wide doors at the entrance to the courtroom. She was in a panic because she knew they had their drama planned, but if the newspapers delivered the evening papers before he could complete his testimony, Hástin Yázhe would, most certainly, be linked to the murder of the young white mother and her child. San Francisco could erupt into vigilante terror, and Mr. Yázhe might be arrested as a possible accomplice or even as the one who gave the orders to his mute assistant.

When they told him he should wear something he wears when he ministers to his tribe, they were not aware of the elaborate nature of the garb. It sounded like a herd of goats with bells on their necks was coming into the room. Upon the top of his head, he had a triangular apparatus with a tall-crowned black hat beneath it. Under that was a mask, divided evenly, black on the right side and white on the other, which covered the two sides of his face. Beneath the mask was the skin of the coyote that she had seen back in Arizona. He wore no shirt, so his dark-brown skin could be seen, and on his chest, beneath a necklace of what resembled Christian crosses, was painted two triangular white swaths of about two-inches wide. Running across his chest, from his right shoulder down to his concho belt, was an inch-wide strip of deer skin laden with silver studs.

Below the waist of his concho belt made of large silver dollars was a skirt made of beads, and then black pants under the skirt. The pant legs were stuffed into high-topped black moccasins. Crow feathers were attached to the outside of the moccasins.

In his right hand he held a crow-feathered rattle with two long-gray streamers. In his left hand he held a three-foot reed-shaped device with different furs and bird feathers decorating it.

Just before he entered the witness box, he turned to the jury. He rattled and shook his accoutrements and lurched forward and backward, as if taunting their presence. When they bounced in their seats, she wondered if they reacted to the exploding lights from the photographers above or from the medicine man's threatening demeanor.

After he was comfortably seated, he took off the mask and allowed the coyote skin to remain encircled around his neck. His face was painted completely white, as if he were mocking the faces that were staring at his strange, aboriginal visage. She approached him carefully, drawing out the tension as Trella Evelyn instructed her to do.

"Mr. Hástin Yázhe, are you not the medicine man of the Navajo tribe's Many Sheep clan? And, were you not graduated from England's Oxford University in 1867 with degrees in Medicine and Religious Studies?" This was the juxtaposed paradox she wanted her audience to assimilate.

Her witness grunted in a deep tone of voice.

"Does that mean affirmative?" She asked. There was nervous laughter in the gallery.

He nodded.

"Was the deceased mother of the victim, Penelope Farmer, a woman named Haseya, a member of your clan? And, did you not treat her for what we in Western medicine call consumption before she died?"

He grunted.

"Mr. Yázhe, we have heard testimony today that points to the fact that your tribal culture believes in skinwalkers, or witches. We who do not have your tradition would like to see how these entities wreak revenge upon their victims. Could you demonstrate for the court how this occurs?"

"Your honor, I object! This is highly unusual and not at all relevant to these legal proceedings." Mr. Stonehill's face was again crimson.

Judge Lattimore stared at her over his spectacles, which were down at the tip of his nose. "Miss Gordon. Excuse me, but your train seems to be straying off the reservation. Could you please guide me once more to your destination?"

She looked up at the judge and smiled. "Your honor, again, I wish to say that I am proving how the victim, Penelope Farmer, may have been subjected to beliefs that are not normal. Her emotions were such that it may have threatened her physical well being on the day in question inside my client's clinic. I merely want to educate the jury as to the specific practices that go on in this tribe, which may have affected Penelope, an impressionable youth."

Lattimore took off his spectacles, extracted a handkerchief from under his robes, and began to clean the lenses. "I need to see this clearly, because my mind is very cloudy at the moment. You may continue with your demonstration, Miss Gordon."

She nodded at the medicine man.

Without uttering a word, or acknowledging her, Hástin Yázhe picked up the mask from his lap and placed it over his hat to cover his face. He climbed down from the witness stand, his tools of witchcraft held aloft, his body stooped over, and he began to sing. It was not a pleasant sound. It began low, in a guttural bass, and slowly rose in both volume and timbre, until it was vibrating in a tremulous tenor. He repeated the same refrain, over and over. It was a single word: *gáagii*.

In his right hand, he began to shake the rattle as he chanted the word. From its insides, a residue cloud of white particles was launched into the air. It began to smell like sulphur, as he leaped about, as if on all fours. He went along the jury panel, screeching at each member and shaking the rattle at him. Some would nervously laugh, a few sneezed from the particles, and one man cursed at the medicine man, raising his fist and shaking it in anger.

After dousing the jury, Hástin slowly turned around, and his chant ceased. He was deathly silent. In what appeared to be a spirit possession, the medicine man began to shake, spin around, and finally fall, on his knees, looking up into the rafters as he did so, his chalk-white face imploring an unseen deity. His arms reached up, shaking the reed-shaped device in his left hand and rattling the feathered gourd in his right.

After being seized with new vigor, he sprang to his feet, and he ran. The Navajo was so silent on his moccasins that no sound of his footsteps could be heard. He was upon her in a few seconds. He reached down to his concho belt and pressed his index finger on the surface of one of the dollars, which opened a tiny drawer. From the drawer he extracted a pinch of powder, as a gentleman might partake of snuff at the opera. Instead of snorting it, he held his pinched-together right thumb and index finger over the head of the defendant, Mrs. Honora Fulbright.

When the particles of powder began to drizzle down upon her body, a crow flew inside one of the open windows in the balcony section. It circled above the courtroom for a few seconds, and then it plummeted downward and landed on the shoulder of the medicine man, cawing raucously, until the defendant suddenly slouched over in her chair, seemingly unconscious to the world of her male persecutors.

Several women screamed in the front rows, and men yelled. The bailiff ran over to seize the medicine man, but Hástin Yázhe raised his right arm, and the bailiff halted, as if he might also become a victim of this unholy cursedness.

The medicine man addressed the bailiff. "Now, can you see? This was powder made from the ground bones of human corpses. This woman would be dead if I were a *yee naaldooshii*, what you call a skinwalker. Is this not true?" He tapped Mrs. Fulbright on the shoulder with his rattle gourd. Her eyes opened slowly, and she sat upright in her chair.

There were gasps and shouts.

"This is corn pollen and not corpse powder," he said, wiping away the residual dust from the defendant's shoulders. "It does not work with corpse powder either. I have tried it. And my friend Lizhini here is a well trained *gáagii*, or crow. He is certainly no evil spirit."

Laura knew that Trella's little drama was being acted out quite nicely. If the final act the medicine man now had to perform worked as well, her case might be won. She recalled what she and Clara had discussed many times about the nature of truth. The truth was never a fact to be revealed through artful syllogism or logic. It was a living experience to be uncovered by human revelation.

She watched the medicine man walk over to her defense table. He set down his tools, took off his black and white mask, and placed it next to them. He then made the long march back toward the witness stand. When he was finally seated, she approached him.

"Do you believe in the powers of these spirits, the skinwalkers?" Her question was forthright and clear.

He looked down at her and drew in his lips before he answered. "No, I do not. In fact, upon every occasion in my practice, I prefer to teach against such superstitious beliefs."

"Is that so? Then how is it you were overheard to remark following a coyote's appearance at Miss Ah Toy's home that the white man needed to be punished for his acts? To quote you, you said, 'They must taste the real revenge of our culture to expose their greed for our land.' What did you mean by that statement, Mr. Yázhe?" She was completing the play with a flourish.

"I simply meant that you do not understand the core of our cultural beliefs. As Dr. McFarland remarked, we take pride in our adaptable teachings and practices. This witchcraft is not part of that. Although, the fact remains that my tribe still believes in these dark forces, and I see it as part of my job to prevent such superstitions. Perhaps it makes me an outcast to many of my own people, but I renounce what Haseya Farmer believed."

She knew there was a contradiction in testimony, and she needed to clarify it before the D. A. took his turn.

"My earlier witness, Mrs. Althea Crutchfield, testified that you told the two women, Mrs. Haseya Farmer and her daughter, Penelope, that they must use their powers to put Mr. Aloysius Farmer back on his proper path as one of the Earth people." She was using the notes she took from Clara's interview of the tutor at the Farmer mansion.

"Mrs. Crutchfield obviously misunderstood my intentions. I knew Haseya believed she was a skinwalker. I could not convince her otherwise, as these beliefs are developed beyond my control, amongst many of the women in my tribe. They also perform abortions, as your women do. Therefore, I used my logic to appeal to her better angels, so to speak. Putting Mr. Farmer on the right path had nothing to do with murder and revenge. Mrs. Crutchfield must have learned those more ominous teachings directly from Haseya after she became ill and was confronted by her husband, who had become angry about something."

"Very well. Then you are aware of the control this superstition can have over some women. Have you seen it do harm in your tribe?" This was the last question she had, and she knew what he was going to say. He had come out with it during their drama rehearsal back at the Toy mansion.

"I most certainly have. These occasions were why I changed my mind concerning such beliefs. One woman had to be confined in the Bureau of Indian Affairs prison at Fort Defiance. She thought she was a wolf, and she killed her aunt, whom she accused of trying to seduce her husband. Another woman, who learned under Haseya, suffered from what Dr. McFarland informed me is called nympho mania. She was under the delusional belief she was a female coyote in heat. Thus, she began to sleep with all the men in her clan. There were other events, such as casting out those women and men who claimed they were *yee naaldooshii*. These people sometimes died alone out in the desert canyons, or they preyed upon other tribal members, or they killed themselves in fits of rage. I could not allow this to continue, but I also could not completely stop it from being believed."

"I understand, Mr. Yázhe. I thank you for your testimony today." She walked back toward her table. "Your witness, Mr. District Attorney," she said.

She saw there was a commotion at the entrance to the courtroom. A uniformed policeman came into the room and hurried over to the prosecution's table. He and Mr. Stonehill exchanged some rather frantic dialogue. If it were what she was thinking, it was not good.

"Mr. Stonehill? Are you ready for your cross examination?" Judge Lattimore tapped his gavel gently on the block.

"Indeed I am, your honor." The Dandy Dan prosecutor

puffed out his chest, and if he were a rooster he would be ready to crow. He approached the medicine man as if he were going to fight him in a cock battle to the death.

"Good day to you, sir. Do you have a mute assistant who came with you from the reservation by the name of Ajei?"

He was certainly not waiting to preface his question. The worst had befallen her cause. Her mind scrambled to find a possible rebuttal.

"Yes, I do." The medicine man was nonplussed. "Has her health gotten worse?"

"Her health, I would wager, is fit. Her mental disposition may not be. She has just been charged with first degree murder."

There were shouts and rumblings throughout the crowded courtroom. Several lights flashed from the press balcony.

She stood up at once. "Your honor, I object. This information is not relevant to my client's case. In point of fact, it can cause undue harm to my witness's own health and safety, and the District Attorney knows it!"

Mr. Stonehill began to pace in a circle that grew ever wider with each turn he made in front of the judge.

"Your honor, this witness is, if you will excuse the expression, hostile. He attempts to declare that he is peace-loving and religious in his activities, and yet his personal assistant has been accused of poisoning a young mother and the babe in her arms, just down the street, inside our own City Hospital. They were both— mother and child--poisoned with the tea the Navajo woman was seen giving to this mother, while she was breastfeeding her child. Shortly thereafter, they began to vomit, tremble, and then collapse. They expired in a grotesque death at three this afternoon."

Judge Lattimore let out a great discharge of air from his lungs. "Counselors, please come forward," he commanded.

She walked with Stonehill up to the bench.

"I want no more references to this suspected murder, Mr. Stonehill. You should have informed me privately of this turn of events. Miss Gordon is correct about endangering the life of this witness. However, the defense witness testimony has become tainted. I will not allow any more testimony from your witness, Miss Gordon. Is that clear? I was too liberal with my allowances already."

She frowned. "Yes, it is quite clear, your honor."

"Very well. I want closing arguments now, if you both don't mind," he said.

They both nodded.

Judge Lattimore instructed the jury to ignore what the prosecutor just said about the other case, and then about what they were to decide in this one. If they decided the defendant was guilty as charged, then they must believe Mrs. Honora Fulbright, on June 20, 1887, acted in her capacity as a midwife to perform a procedure on the victim, Miss Penelope Farmer, which they judge to be a negligent act. This act must amount to a wanton and reckless disregard of the victim's safety and the possible consequences. The prosecution must have proved to them, beyond any reasonable doubt, and with a majority of the evidence, that this negligence existed and was the direct cause of the death of Miss Farmer.

She had her closing speech planned, and this was her last moment to raise all the doubts she had presented and fix them into the minds of these male jurors.

"Miss Gordon? You may present your closing argument," Judge Lattimore instructed.

She walked over to stand in front of the jury panel. She was not a pacer the way her friend Clara was. Her voice was deep for a woman, a contralto in a choir. She was ashamed of it when she was married, but when she became an attorney it became an asset. She also did not use notes when she concluded. This was when she used her emotional appeals, and as a defense attorney, she knew that reasonable doubt was emotionally based in the human psyche.

"Gentlemen of jury. Before you render your considered verdict, I want to go over what I have covered on my client's behalf these two days. Please remember that I have no burden of proof. This is what is required of the State. All I must do is to make reasonable arguments about how the facts you know can be seen differently. This difference, in legal terms, is called reasonable doubt. Would a reasonable man, in the same situation as you, doubt that such an extreme variety of negligence took place?"

She pointed over to her client, Mrs. Fulbright. The jurors' eyes followed her motion to stare at the woman.

"Mrs. Honora Fulbright has practiced as a midwife for over ten years. She has never been accused of any malfeasance or legal infraction before. She has never performed an abortion with the surgical instruments about which we described during this trial. In point of fact, she is not an abortionist, in the strict sense of the term. She does, from time to time, refer women to surgeons who do perform abortions. The reality is, gentlemen, that her main clientele are women who are Chinese and who have more faith in the oriental medical system. So, she uses abortifacients and other drugs to continue menstrual flow, as well as the pressure acupuncture process that was demonstrated by the prosecution in this case."

She noticed that Mr. Stonehill was shaking his head and frowning. That was a positive sign.

"I shall admit to you, gentlemen, that both the District Attorney and I presented some theatrics for you to contemplate. I did not know he was presenting a Chinese drama, and he certainly was not aware of my medicine man demonstration. However, I want to argue that his presentation had less to do with the charge against my client than mine did. Why? First of all, when Miss Penelope Farmer, the victim, contacted Mrs. Fulbright, she was in a panicked and emotionally unstable condition. Without any previous contact or examination, my client agreed to see her simply because Miss Farmer was in pain, and it was obviously an emergency. What did Mrs. Fulbright do inside her clinic? She gave her patient a legal pain reliever, sold over the counter in thousands of pharmacies in the United States. In addition, because the girl requested it, Mrs. Fulbright did perform the pressure procedure to her body."

The jurors were nodding. Some stared down at the notes they had taken, others made new notes as she spoke.

"I submit a logical and reasonable alternative to the requirement of extreme negligence that my client is accused of committing. Honora Fulbright did not know Penelope had an ectopic pregnancy. This fact was revealed after the girl's death. Therefore, would a reasonable person say Mrs. Fulbright was required to perform a surgical procedure to examine the girl, keeping in mind she was in extreme pain, and this was an emergency? I say not, gentleman. I say, in point of fact, that it was more reasonable to assume that it was this rare and aberrational physical and mental condition of the patient which caused her death. The mental delusion was that she believed she was a skinwalker, as Dr. McFarland, Mr. Yázhe, and Mrs. Crutchfield testified she was under the spell of her mother, Haseya. Mrs. Honora Fulbright did not cause this ectopic pregnancy, did she? She did not fill her patient's mind with the horrific tales of skinwalkers or make her believe she was haunted by her mother's spirit. No. She did not. My client was simply attempting to relieve the pain of her patient and perform a non-surgical practice upon her body. Would you, gentlemen, if you were a midwife with my client's expertise, want to assist somebody in pain, in an emergency? Is that reasonable? Yes. It is. It is not reasonable, however, to believe you would then be responsible for the death that ensued. I want to give you a final metaphorical comparison to fix in your mind as you deliberate."

The jury members were staring fixedly at her, their pencils and pens at the ready like good students. She hoped the journalists in the balcony were also ready to get an accurate statement of what she was about to say.

"Suppose I am a gentleman, just like one of you. I am feeling pain in my chest, but I don't know its cause. I am also under the mental delusion that my wife has poisoned me. I go to a hospital that is approved by the American Medical Association. A receiving doctor, a General Practitioner, listens to my story, and he then takes my vital signs. He knows about my extreme pain, and he knows about my accusation concerning my wife. The doctor treats me for the possible poisoning, but he does not investigate the real cause, which is a blocked artery, an embolism. If I die, is it reasonable to charge this physician with negligence because he did not investigate the actual cause of my death? Think about that analogy, gentlemen. I believe it's fair, and perhaps you can see how it relates to the unreasonable involuntary manslaughter charge for which my client is now accused. This is not a case about morality, nor is it a case about pagan medicine practiced without a license. My client was fully authorized to practice what she did as a midwife, and she did what any reasonable person in her professional capacity would do. She did not, however, perform any direct act upon the body of Penelope Farmer to cause her death. Thank you for your service, gentlemen of the jury. I hope you make the rational decision in favor of my client's innocence."

When the second policeman broke through the double-doors, and ran up to the judge, she was prepared for the worst. Judge Lattimore, after listening for several moments, again motioned for her and Mr. Stonehill to come to his bench.

"There has been another murder. This time your associate, Mrs. Foltz, is directly involved," he said, staring down at her.

"How can that be? She did not kill anyone, did she?" Her heart was racing at the macabre possibility Clara was involved in a homicide.

"No. I'm afraid the victim is Mrs. Foltz's civil client, and the father of our victim, Mr. Aloysius Farmer."

Chapter 12: Four Corners

The Toy Mansion, Fifteen Nob Hill, San Francisco, July 8, 1887.

The jury's deliberation in the trial of Mrs. Honora Fulbright took two hours. Their verdict, to the group assembled in the library the day following, was rather unimportant, even though Laura's client was declared innocent of involuntary manslaughter. What was more important to the stability of a city gone wild in the press with rumors of "vicious savages taking retribution upon innocent citizens," and "street vigilantes meeting to take their own brand of vengeance," was the singular and quite suspicious response to the editorial Clara published in her *San Diego Daily Bee*, which she received the day before. It was this missive she wanted to discuss.

Clara surveyed the investigative team she assembled following the horrific aftermath of the murders of her client, Aloysius Farmer, and the mother and child at San Francisco City Hospital. Seated to her left were Laura Gordon, Ah Toy, Captain Isaiah Lees, Dr. Andrew McFarland, and Trella Evelyn. To her right were the Claflin sisters, Victoria and Tennessee, Navajo Medicine Man, Hástin Yázhe, and his assistant, Ajei, newly released from imprisonment. At the back of the room stood her son, Samuel Cortland, and his betrothed, Adeline Quantrill.

The day before, she had attempted to question the tutor, Mrs. Crutchfield, and the chauffeur, Edward Barnes, at the Farmer residence, but they were out of town. She was able to obtain information from Victoria about whom to call at Oxford University's medical school to discuss Hástin Yázhe's training. What she uncovered from her inquiries was enough to make her request this emergency meeting.

"My friends, there are strange events happening, and I will share with you the relevant facts which the San Francisco Police have determined concerning the three murders. Captain Lees, who was at the scenes of both crimes, and who knows what the forensics people have determined, shall explain."

She nodded at Isaiah, and he stood up. He wore his usual detective outfit of a brown frock coat and vest with checkered pants and spit-shined Oxfords. He looked down at the reports he extracted from a folder.

"Ajei was cleared of all charges. At first, she was assumed to be responsible for the deaths of the mother, Mrs. Edwina Temple and her child Lorena, because she gave the mother tea while she was breastfeeding her infant. It was assumed a poison in the tea had been imbibed by the mother and passed on to her child. This, as determined by chemistry analysis, was not the cause."

"Then why was she arrested?" Laura asked.

"It was logical. She was the nearest possible suspect. However, it was later determined after the autopsy was performed that the tea had no poison content. Some great fear in the mind of the mother caused her to smother her child in the blanket."

"My goodness! What would make a mother do that?" Victoria extracted a fan from her handbag and began to flutter it in front of her face.

"Dr. Snow said this happens when a person is so horrified that it triggers the autonomic system's release of increased adrenaline. It is the fight-or-flight reflex. The mother, before she expired, and after she asphyxiated her baby, experienced a rapid heart rate, dilated pupils, and increased blood flow to the muscles. After adrenaline is released, Dr. Snow said, calcium rushes into the heart cells, which causes the heart muscle to contract in a massive response. The calcium keeps pouring in, and the heart muscle can't relax, which causes an arrhythmia called ventricular fibrillation."

"She died from fright," Dr. McFarland said.

"Quite so, doctor."

"What about my client, Mr. Farmer? How did he die?" Clara asked. She was mentally connecting what was said in her newspaper letter to the editor to what Captain Lees was saying.

Isaiah's face winced. "He was not as fortunate, I am afraid. He was discovered within his abortifacient storeroom. His throat had been opened by the canines of some large animal. Indeed. Parts of his stomach and his right leg had also been devoured. Dr. Snow found the fur around his body of what was determined to be that of a large wolf."

"Wolf? What of the coyotes we have been hearing? I heard one at his mansion when I was questioning the staff," Clara said.

"No. Snow was insistent that it was a timber wolf." Isaiah wiped his sweating brow with a handkerchief he took from his frock coat pocket. "There was something else. There were bloody footprints inside the storeroom. However, these obvious wolf paw impressions led to the door. But extending from the door out into the hallway were the prints of a barefoot human—the size of a male adult."

Ajei began to sing in a high-pitched voice.

Hástin Yázhe placed his hand on her shoulder and she stopped. "*Yee naaldooshii,*" he said, in a harsh whisper.

Laura turned in her chair to confront him. "What did you just say? You told us all under oath that these skinwalkers were superstitious inventions. You said they did not exist and that you were attempting to eradicate these witches and their beliefs from your tribe's culture. Are you a hypocritical, lying bastard?"

She began to strike the muscular native on his chest with both her fists. He allowed her to do so, and yet it did not change his serious demeanor. After she tired, the medicine man exhaled and stared up at the ceiling.

"Many of my people believe there are places where the powers of both good and evil are present and that these powers can be harnessed for either. Medicine men like myself utilize these powers to heal and aid members of their communities, while those who practice Navajo witchcraft seek to direct the spiritual forces to inflict harm or misfortune upon others. This type of Navajo witchcraft is known as the Witchery Way, which uses human corpses in various ways such as tools from the bones, and other concoctions that are used to curse, harm, or kill intended victims."

Clara cleared her throat. "Thank you, Mr. Yázhe. I know you probably don't believe in these witchery practices, but in light of what's happened, we must assume the worst. I want to share a letter I received concerning the editorial I wrote in my newspaper. It may shine some rather strange light upon our current mystery."

"Yes, please do. All of the other responses to our opinion pieces were either angry rebuttals or accusations that we side with the heathen hordes of savages," Tennessee said. "I, for one, am not a savage," she added.

Clara extracted a piece of paper from a folder on the library table and began to read:

You say the Navajo people and their culture deserve to be protected from harm. That is not what is true. Instead of protection your government and people are chasing our tribes away from the holy ways. We, who have assembled at the Four Corners, must show you our powers, the same way you show us yours. For each woman who leaves our tribe to join your infestation of machines and madness, we shall kill one of yours. For each child born thereafter, born into your government of treachery, lies and deceit, we shall steal one of yours. For each line you make on our land and declare it to be one of your states, we shall haunt you at your window, attack you in your sleep, and slaughter your animals. For this is the way of the Collective of yee naaldooshii. For this is the way of the Truth that is from the grave. If you wish to see our powers, then come to the Four Corners and behold our magnificence!

In the back of the room, Adeline Quantrill, the young psychic, began to weave in place and swoon. Her eyes rolled back into their sockets until the two orbs were pearl white. When she spoke, it was a language she did not understand, but Clara knew who did. After the ranting, high-pitched tirade was finally over, she turned toward the medicine man.

"Was that your native tongue?" she asked.

"It was," he replied.

"Can you translate it for us?" She knew their collective path was turning toward a shadow reality that she really did not want to explore, but from what she now knew, they must appreciate how many more lives might be lost if they ignored what was happening around them.

"The entity speaking through this girl says he is in the Four Corners Coven. The spirit of Haseya enters me, she says. I can lock eyes with them. Possess them. Force them to see a vision that explodes their hearts. I can change, in a flash. I keep my human sight inside the wolf. They flash light upon my eyes, and my eyes turn red. I have to escape under the cover of fog and night. Stay away from Four Corners if you value your life and your soul!"

She watched Samuel place an arm around his beloved to comfort her. Adeline was exhausted and shaking from the channeling, if that's what it was. How else could she speak a language she had never used or learned? Her parents, it was true, were murdered by Apaches on the train ride across the plains to San Francisco. That was the young woman's only experience with native culture. This channeling meant a very powerful spiritual presence was invading her psyche.

This was not their first confrontation with the supernatural. The case of the spiritualist murders introduced her and her family to the clairvoyant orphan, Adeline, and she became an important part of solving that mystery. In the Stockton Insane asylum investigation, Mrs. Elizabeth Packard and Dr. McFarland showed her how the mind could be manipulated for evil purposes. Then, earlier this year, in Washington D. C., during the case of the Supreme Court nominee's assassination, they confronted another group of evil manipulators, bigots, and kidnappers who worshipped the ancient god Mithras.

"Ladies and gentlemen. This will be our chance to uncover the truly murderous side of aboriginal paranormal revenge. I want to pursue this case to its conclusion, but I have another financial dilemma. If I am to move to San Diego next year, I cannot afford to travel to Four Corners." She already told her family about her move, but her guests were unaware.

Victoria and her sister Tennessee stood up and looked at each other. They nodded before speaking, and Victoria made the speech.

"Our career and financial successes were forged by the power from the unknown. Without the supernatural, we women would still be forced to be alone and separate, tending to our womanly chores for men. This is, most likely, our final opportunity

145

to experience real exhilaration and adventure, and we want to help you in your endeavor, Mrs. Foltz. Whatever money you need to finance this trip, consider it donated from us, in the name of female liberation and cooperation. What can we do to combat these monsters of Darwin's evolutionary curse?"

Clara looked over at the medicine man once more. "Mr. Yázhe, we have no human suspects at this time. To uncover the truth and to stop more of these murders from taking place, we must know if there is a way to confront our adversaries with any chance of victory over them. Are you willing to tell us more about what we can do, and if you can indeed lead us into Four Corners territory?"

The tall dark man seemed uncomfortable. He fidgeted at his necklace of silver coins with his hands. He looked over at his assistant and then turned back to face the white people.

"I feel responsible for what has happened, and this is why I agree to escort you to Four Corners. But first, let me tell you about what I know. You must promise to never divulge this information to anybody outside of this room or to discuss it amongst yourselves after we go there. Is that a solemn promise on your lives?"

Clara watched all nine of the white people nod their heads, as did she. This was another moment of a much different kind of truth.

"The evil society of the witches gathers in dark caves or secluded places for several purposes--to initiate new members, plot their activities, harm people from a distance with black magic, and perform dark ceremonial rites. These ceremonies are similar to other tribal affairs, including dancing, feasts, rituals, and sand-painting, but they are corrupted with dark connotations." The medicine man saw Dr. McFarland raise his hand, and he nodded toward him.

"These are medicine people who left their different tribes to go to the Four Corners, correct? They did not have faith in the way you and your other brethren practiced your craft."

"Very true. They began to do this after your armies destroyed and looted our villages, murdered our brethren, and forced us on long marches. I may be a spirit leader who knows the ways of your people, but these skinwalkers have gone over to an evil side that is unimaginable to our ways."

Samuel spoke up from the back of the room. "How much more evil can they be? It seems that what they've already done is in the realm of Edgar Allan Poe and his most horrific tales."

"That is a good comparison. These evil doers are known to engage in necrophilia with female corpses, eat the flesh of humans, commit incest, and rob graves to steal jewelry and to acquire their tools of infamy. Perhaps your Mr. Poe has never imagined such evil."

Trella Evelyn raised her hand, and he nodded toward her.

"What other powers do they allegedly possess? What will we be facing?"

"They can read minds and control others' thoughts and behaviors, as was the instance at your public hospital."

Adeline spoke up. "Read minds? They are also telepathic?"

"Yes. During these gatherings, the skinwalkers shape-shift into their animal forms or go about naked, wearing only beaded jewelry and ceremonial paint. Much the way I was dressed in the courtroom. Their leader is, most likely, a very old man, who is a powerful and acrimonious judge of what they all do. If we can pursue him and kill or arrest him, then we may be able to halt what is happening."

Ah Toy spoke from her seat. "Why have you not confronted them before? Will this be the first time you have visited Four Corners?"

He looked over at her and he frowned. "We Navajo did attempt to eradicate our witches in the 1878 Witch Purge. In college, I learned of your similar attempts earlier, during the Salem, Massachusetts witch trials. Many braves rode to Four Corners area, which then was not called by that name, and determined who were Navajo among them. There were forty such witches, and we killed them all to restore harmony and balance for our tribe. But when our enemies, both from other tribes and you whites, began to harass us once more, other medicine men became evil and joined their compatriots in the valley of destruction and infamy."

Captain Lees spoke up. "I have a question of the moment,"

147

he said, fingering the handle of his Colt .45 around his waist. "How does one kill a skinwalker?"

Mr. Yázhe nodded his head. "I know some spells and rituals that can turn the skinwalker's evil back upon itself. Another option is to shoot the creature, after it has shifted, with bullets dipped in white corpse ash, made from the human bones of its victims."

"Victims? You mean . . .?" Clara was not able to bring herself to complete the sentence.

"Yes. I'm afraid so, Mrs. Foltz," the medicine man said. He turned back to the captain. "Can you do this?"

"If that's the only way, then I shall do it," Captain Lees said, moving toward the door. "Include me on your trip's roster, Clara. I will return after I have paid a visit to the City Morgue. I will bring prepared bullets and pistols for everyone. When are we leaving?" He turned to her while standing at the library door.

"Are you all going?" Her eyes scanned the audience of brave hearts and gentle people. Each one raised a hand.

Only Adeline seemed hesitant at first. "I fear what will happen when my mind confronts any of these creatures," she said.

"That will not be problematic," said the medicine man. "They will read your mind, but you will not be able to read theirs, unless they are dead, like Haseya."

"I shall purchase train fare for twelve to leave the day after tomorrow, July 10. We should be at Four Corners in four days from now. I shall see you all at the station. May God be with us." Clara moved toward the exit, and the others followed her.

"One more thing," said Mr. Yázhe. "These creatures can also control lightening, under certain weather conditions."

"We can circumvent that when the time comes," said Captain Lees, smiling. "Although, I am not as fast on my feet as I used to be," he added.

Four Corners of the Territories of Arizona, Utah, New Mexico and the State of Colorado. July 12, 1887.

I don't know why I agreed to go on this journey to the Four

Corners. The very thought of actually seeing one of these creatures was seizing my imagination with a fright from which I could not escape. All the way out to our destiny, I could not speak one word. Instead, my eyes kept moving from one male member of our group to the next. I believed only these four men could save us, so all my attention was upon their every word and every plan. It was as if my suffragette demeanor vanished, and I was once more the frightened little girl watching her Civil War veteran father leave her family forever in San Jose.

I recalled the way Captain Lees described how the young mother had been frightened to death by something she was forced to see. I was afraid to shut my eyes because I might see that same vision, so I stared straight ahead, my eyes fixed upon the back of my brother Samuel's head.

Only these men could save me from being ravaged by a skinwalker, my mind possessed, forcing me to jump from the ledge of a mountain, or to embrace a venomous snake to my bosom like Cleopatra. Somehow, all the other powers of these witches were not as frightening. Only this singular ability to take over my thoughts caused me to feel a panic beyond description.

I wondered why mother had become so persuaded by this Navajo and his explanations. Even though she had always accepted Adeline's telepathy and autobiographical memory, mother usually stopped short at black magic or the phantasmagorical reality of creatures like the skinwalkers.

During our train trip, Mr. Yázhe gradually took over his role as our guide and leader. He handed out necklaces, with pieces of human bone threaded upon them, for us to wear. He said they would distract the creatures when they shifted into some animal form and pursued us. The closer the train got us to the point of no return, with the rural wastelands of the Navajo and Ute Nations encircling us, like the nature of truth itself, the more our leader spoke of the signs we might notice to show that an evil medicine man was nearby.

"They can run along with a train like this," he said, pointing out the car's window to the passing scenery of cacti and scrub pine, as we sped along the rails on the Durango Silverton Narrow Gauge

Railroad. This line took us from Durango, Colorado out to the Four Corners station.

"A skinwalker enjoys jumping up on the cars or peering at you through windows. Like the coyote, they are often tricksters, hiding a piece of your jewelry or tickling your hair while you sleep. You can often feel the ground tremble when they are running nearby."

I was enraptured by his tales of the supernatural, and the nearer we got to our destination, the more adornments he would drape around his own neck, or stick inside his deerskin jacket, his vest pocket, and his trousers. He had potions and salves, lockets and gourd rattles, and many other items that appeared to be parts of animals. I imagined if I did survive, I might create a wonderful stage play about my experiences. I know my drama department friends at Berkeley would certainly enjoy my story, as their minds are filled with the likes of Shakespeare, Marlow, Oscar Wilde, Wilkie Collins, and Charles Dickens. A drama about the hunt for the *yee naaldooshii* would make me very popular, indeed, especially with Terrance Saylor, my new beau.

I am writing in this journal to keep my mind occupied, lest it be held captive by my greatest fear. As we pull into the Four Corners Junction, the Navajo informs us we shall take a buckboard out to the valley to arrive before night descended upon us. The thought of camping out there in the wilderness made my skin crawl, and my heart quickened its beat.

As we climbed into the buckboard driven by two horses, I noticed a commotion outside the small trading post at the station. Five policemen from the Bureau of Indian Affairs were rounding up three drunken natives and pushing them toward a waiting horse cart which bore the BIA insignia on its side. Captain Lees walked over to the group, and tapped the leader of the police, a white man, on the shoulder. I saw him turn, and he seemed to recognize Mr. Lees, and they shook hands. As my mother's lover returned to climb aboard, I looked at the captain's gun inside his holster and the Bowie knife encased in the sheath around his chest. I finally breathed a sigh of relief, as we began our journey out into the vast wilderness of the

Indian Nation.

Four hours later, in the bloodless valley near the Great Sand Dunes.

Clara watched her eldest daughter, Trella Evelyn, as she climbed down from the buckboard. She seemed awkward and tentative in her movements, and her motherly instincts understood she needed to keep a watchful eye on her. Mr. Yázhe was pointing to a cave up ahead, near the sand dunes. She could see the tall Mount Blanca in the distance, standing guard, its snow-covered peak, even in summer, covered with a white mantle like an old Indian woman with white hair stretched out on an earthy divan. They all wore Levis, flannel shirts, and hiking boots with wide, floppy-brimmed prospectors' hats. There was no female attire suitable for these environs.

The abnormal sounds and odors of the evening were beginning to encroach upon their senses. Out in this wilderness, away from the city, their ears were alert, their noses were keen, and their eyes might spring out of their sockets at the first sound of a rustling bush, the screech of a cougar, or the howl of a wolf. In her mind's eye, she could still picture her client, Mr. Farmer, his throat slashed, his body devoured. However, she also knew she had come to this place because of her own theory of what it might hold in the way of final truth.

"They call it the bloodless valley because of the many tribes who worship these mountains and this land. We never fought here, but perhaps this is why our outcasts, the skinwalkers, came here after we were attacked back home. They believed this land held some healing elixir to soothe their ravaged minds. Alas, they grew apart and afraid, and their beliefs strayed from the holy path of truth. They say these great sand dunes were formed from the earth at the bottom of the Rio Grande, when it was without water and was blown by the winds, many thousands of years ago. My brother medicine men became insane with revenge, and they also swept into this valley to engorge it with their dark magic."

She knew they were the strangers, so her group followed

their guide back into the shadows of the dunes and into a small opening in a nearby hill, etched into the red earth like a natural shrine. The fluttering of bats' wings greeted them as they walked in a line through the narrow entrance and down into the tunnel leading to a wide cavern below. The stalactites and stalagmites—pointed daggers of minerals deposits hanging down from the ceiling, and round-topped cudgels growing up from the earth—were right next to a running stream that was glistening under the light of the gas lantern Captain Lees held in his right hand. In his other hand, he held his Colt pistol, with its magical bullets.

The twelve of them, like apostles to Nature, spread out blankets and pillows to sleep for the night. Their guide informed them it was best to wait until early morning to hunt for the witches, as they were most vulnerable then, in their mountain caves, afraid of the gathering light of a new dawn. He said he and Captain Lees would hunt down the leader of the skinwalkers and bring him back to this cave, alive or dead. They would be safe here tonight, as he was going to stand watch.

Mr. Yázhe poured out liquid into eleven clam shells contained in a jug he extracted from his duffle bag. He told them it was a naturally soothing tonic to help them sleep in these strange environs. He had a potion for himself that would allow him to get rest even though his eyes remained open. Ajei sang a soft melody that drifted over their reclining bodies in a comforting refrain.

As she gradually fell asleep, she pictured her five children frolicking inside the cavern's prehistory. Their moving shadows were animated figures in a show made just for her. When she was awakened, along with her friends, they were forced to stand up, groggy from their drugged sleep, and the world was still dark. She felt the thick cloth around her head, and her hands were tied together in the small of her back, and her pure consciousness knew it had finally begun.

Chapter 13: Truth Revealed

Front-page Editorial in the San Diego Daily Bee, July 15, 1887.

The Publisher, my mother, Clara Shortridge Foltz, Esquire, has awarded me this task of explaining what occurred on that fateful day of July 12 in the wilds of Navajo and Ute country called the Four Corners. As the Editor-in-Chief, she has also read my missive and given her final approval. Her words will live with me forever, as I pursue my personal dreams of becoming an actress and perhaps an author for the dramatic stage:

"You must entitle your editorial 'The Nature of Truth,' Trella. This will give you the impetus to remember what actually took place, and it will also allow you to see how like an onion reality truly is. It is we who peel back the layers of our experience, gradually, with our memories. And, as one peels back this odorous metaphor, we ultimately find that it reveals . . . nothing. For nothing lies at the center of the nature of truth because the authentic truth, my daughter, lies in the knowledge of discovery during the act of peeling away."

We both are aware that our competitors in the world of journalism are featuring all of the more controversial elements of this story. We also know that the profits from our competitors' versions of our story are far greater, and far more unbelievable, at least to us who were actually there. Therefore, as we were the ten who were personally involved, we respectfully admonish these fictions. In the world of proper legal and journalism research, the crown jewel goes to those witnesses who were present. Even with this crown, one who is a true student of philosophical reality knows, the one who experiences can also be deluded, by and for many reasons: profit, insanity, bias, and power, to name just a few.

I truly wish I were creating a play for you, such as I did for my family in *Water*, which was also a dramatic treatise on the nature of reality. However, in art, which is not appreciated in life, characters and what they do and say reach symbolic and metaphoric levels, so as not to confront the "baser" realities of politics and the fear of being different. I shall focus upon the reality that I know, and it is based upon the research of my mother and her friends, and upon the acceptance of differences between cultures, and even the differences of the realities which exist between those in the same cultures. Remember that onion, my dear reader, and you will survive my missive intact with your intelligence, such as that may be.

When we awakened the morning after our arrival at the cave next to the Great Dunes, in the bloodless valley, on July 12, 1887, all ten of us had been kidnapped, to use the legal term. To arrive at this conundrum, we had been, I realize after the fact, tricked by the very father of trickery, Mr. Hástin Yázhe. I had not, however, foreseen the intelligent mental deviousness of my mother. I thought we were all doomed, and Mr. Yázhe, whose fantastic tales of the Skinwalkers, the *yee naaldooshii*, had mesmerized my young imagination to the point of hypnosis.

There we were, as Dickens would phrase it, confronted by our captors. They were not, however, at all the way they had been described to us in Mr. Yázhe's colloquy. All of the black magic, shape-shifting, and mind control magic were not present. After our hoods were removed, we saw that this was a group of merely seven. Five gentlemen, who, except for our host and chief trickster and his assistant, were attired in the basic uniform of the Western outdoorsman and, dare I say, cowboy. Levis, flannel shirts, and hats that befit men telling tales of the range by a campfire. There were two women, one of whom was white. When I read some of the stories in the other newspapers, I was fascinated by the descriptions of the "savage nakedness" and "bloodthirsty dancing around the campfire" that occurred, which we, who were present, never experienced. Perhaps their information came from the host, who was, most assuredly, full of such tales.

No, his speech to us, compared to his earlier dramatics, even inside the courtroom, was brief in the extreme and to the point. He told us we were now his hostages and that he was going to reap a great bounty from our captivity. Once he had received the monetary gain, we would be released, and he would be moving on to places unknown. I am sorry if that speech does not meet with your fertile imagination of what these pagans are supposedly capable of doing. It certainly did not meet with my fantasies. Therefore, when I explain to you how my genius *materfamilias* was able to deduce how this kidnapping had come to its inglorious fruition, you may be as amazed as I was.

Eight of our group of ten, it seems, had been fooled completely. At least, after I interviewed them, they told me they were as bedazzled and taken in by the medicine man as I was. Most sadly, perhaps it was our good friend, and my mother's law partner, Laura Gordon, who was the most crestfallen. Indeed. After the facts came out, it was her reputation that may have become the most endangered by the next layer of onion I shall reveal. She has given me permission to explain it, as she is, after all, an attorney who seeks truth, above all else, and it with this noble spirit that I relate the following crucial part of my story.

Perhaps the cruelest truth we uncovered was that the young girl, Penelope Farmer, had been kept drugged with peyote and heroin for many years. Hástin Yázhe did this with members of his tribe who needed to be kept close to him, dependant upon him for more than just their physical and spiritual health. Ajei, Mrs. Gordon's lover, was one of these dependent ones, so he knew it could work. He prescribed this hallucinatory medicine for the girl after her mother returned to the reservation and was coughing up blood. Mrs. Crutchfield and Mr. Barnes agreed. The girl could be kept in a state of complete confusion and dependency. The skinwalker myth would become that much more real, and the sex with her father would become what they told her it was. She had become possessed by her mother's spirit.

He had, in point of fact, used that same mesmerizing and medicating skill upon his entire tribe, and, most especially, upon the key figures in his overall ruse to gain profit, Haseya and Penelope Farmer, as well as Mrs. Althea Crutchfield and Mr. Edward Barnes.

Our journalism competitors have seized upon different angles of our story, which have nothing to do with the reality of the people involved in the actual experience. For example, Miss Ajei, the young mute woman who was the medicine man's assistant, manipulated Laura de Force Gordon sexually in order to get into her good graces. Some journalists have condemned both the Navajo woman and the attorney for their consensual and sexual relationship. They have concocted ideas that Mrs. Gordon and the young Navajo were both taking heroin, and other hypnotic drugs, so they could enjoy their bacchanalian trysts that much better. This is not true. These reporters might have been taking these drugs as well, as they completely forget about the power dynamic of that courtship and its ultimate purpose. The purpose of the two criminals, the medicine man and his assistant, was to frighten their white community of naïve humans so much, and to manipulate them in any way possible, so as to more smoothly evolve into the horrific kidnappers that they became. I am getting ahead of my story, however, so let me go back in time to that morning when we peeled away that first layer of dark onion.

The gossip in the San Francisco press was true. Attorney Gordon was having a physical relationship with the mute assistant, Ajei, and she was also taken in by the lies of one of her trial's key witnesses, our master of kidnapping, Hástin Yázhe. Perhaps Mrs. Gordon is the most tragic victim of this entire story, as she beseeches you all to attempt to understand her life and her predicament. When I explain how Mrs. Gordon was being used, as all eight of us were, to a greater and lesser degree, being used, then you may take pity upon her.

The fact is, Miss Ajei's very life may, in the near future, be in Mrs. Gordon's highly capable, defense attorney hands, or perhaps in my mother's. For such is the state of legal reality in my society's tribe. Women, at the very least, are not to be taken seriously, and are always to be suspected of the most monstrous deeds—especially when it concerns our bodies and our minds. The truth is, it was Mrs. Crutchfield who related these conspiracies to my mother and to attorney Gordon, so one may assume the wider conspiracy was shared amongst the four major conspirators, even the two men.

The medicine man and Ajei, along with their co-conspirators, Mrs. Althea Crutchfield and Mr. Edward Barnes, had first planned their scheme when Mr. Yázhe's understudy, Haseya

Farmer, left the Navajo reservation to live with her new husband, Aloysius, in San Francisco. Mr. Farmer was singled out for his wealth as an abortifacient merchant. The moral issue of abortion did not concern the conspirators, however, although we shall be hearing their version of these events in due time, in a courtroom, and their story, I would assume, will change dramatically. Thanks to our First Amendment, I am able to share these facts beforehand.

According to my mother and Captain of Detectives, Mr. Isaiah Lees, the plan these conspirators initially had grew wider, and more audacious, the more they succeeded, as each layer of their dark onion was revealed to them. Acquiring the money was the first layer. Mrs. Crutchfield and Mr. Barnes agreed to perpetrate the hoax involving the mother's child, Penelope Farmer. When the mother, Haseya, contracted fatal consumption, rather than leaving this world without revenge, both personal and tribal, Mr. Yázhe, Mrs. Crutchfield and Mr. Barnes decided upon a devious plan. They were to convince Penelope that she was seduced by her father, utilizing the tribe's superstitious legend of the Skinwalkers and a variety of drugs from the medicine man's pharmacy as mind control methods. In reality, it was Mr. Yázhe who impregnated the girl while she was in an unconscious, drugged state. The drugs she was given, and the tales she was told about her father were all that she remembered. To this moment, we do not know if her father even molested her, or if the girl were having horrible hallucinations.

However, after Penelope proved to be an imaginative and quite gullible victim, on all accounts, Mrs. Crutchfield concocted another scheme whereby the father, Mr. Farmer, and the midwife, Mrs. Honora Fulbright, would be accused of the rape and subsequent death of Penelope Farmer. At first, the pregnant girl Penelope was to be murdered by suprarenal injection, about which I will explain later as concerns the deaths of the mother and child in the maternity ward. When it was discovered, upon drugging of the pregnant fifteen-year-old by Mr. Barnes, and the subsequent physical examination of her uterus by Mr. Yázhe and Mrs. Crutchfield, that Penelope was in danger from an ectopic pregnancy, the death by injection was, as a result, kept as an alternative plan.

Mrs. Crutchfield, who was one of the board members of the orphan asylum charities, stood to gain a lot of money if her lawsuit were victorious over Mr. Farmer. My mother, of course, was chosen by Mr. Farmer to defend him in this case, and Mrs. Fulbright chose Mrs. Gordon as her defense attorney. As we know now, the second civil trial that my mother was to argue never took place. It was these murders of both Mr. Farmer and the young mother and her breastfeeding child, inside the public hospital, which led mother to investigate further into their specific circumstances.

Therefore, the onion was peeled back, but my mother had yet to see the other layers until she searched on her own. She realized, following her research, that the resulting plan mother concocted--once it was scheduled--required the cooperation of her entire group. This led the rest of us, sans Detective Lees, her paramour, into her plan, but we were required to be kept quite ignorant of what she had concluded.

After Attorney Gordon won her case in court, Mr. Yázhe decided it was too risky to pin all of their monetary hopes on the civil trial, especially after seeing the skill of the defense attorney. His dark onion was peeled once more. The conspirators believed my mother would be that much more motivated, so they came up with the idea of using the Skinwalker Legend once more to bring their grand kidnapping ruse to complete fruition. My mother peeled back her layer of the truth onion when the young mother was murdered inside the maternity ward of the San Francisco Public Hospital.

Although fascinated with the story the medicine man gave them about how these Skinwalkers could capture the mind of the young mother and cause her to kill both her infant and herself, she did not find it truthful. As a mother of five children, she said afterward, she did not trust the tale at its core, even though she believes women capable of extremely evil acts, as proved to be the case with Miss Ajei. The truth was revealed about the hospital murders when my mother called Oxford Medical School in London and discussed what Mr. Yázhe had studied during his schooling there in the 1860s.

Mother discovered that the Navajo had studied under Dr.

Thomas Addison, who had, in 1849, published a paper that said there was a disease of the suprarenal capsules, from which he deduced there might be a method of extracting the contents of these glands above the kidneys to analyse its effects upon animals. Mr. Yázhe, as a graduate assistant, injected these animals with the liquid from the suprarenals, and he discovered they could cause the death of the animals, who exhibited the same symptoms that were exhibited in the death of Mrs. Temple, the young mother, in the hospital murder.

During my mother's speech to us about going with the Navajo and his assistant to Four Corners, she and Detective Lees knew the truth about these forensic findings of the mother's death. The symptoms they described to the press were true. It was as if the woman had succumbed to fright. However, the careful inspection of the body by Captain Lees' forensics doctor showed the needle mark of a fresh injection, on the bottom of the right large toe of the woman. Mother realized that this needle injection was what Mr. Yázhe had done during his studies at Oxford's School of Medicine. Therefore, the young woman had not been frightened to death. She was given an injection of the powerful suprarenal gland. The death of the infant, it was surmised, was probably accomplished by suffocation, yes, but by the hands of Ajei, and not by her mother.

As for the murder of Mr. Farmer, I must return to the morning we awoke to our captors inside the cave. There were of course the four major conspirators, whom I have already mentioned, the Navajo medicine man, Mr. Yázhe, and his drug addict assistant, the mute, Ajei, as well as Mrs. Crutchfield and Mr. Barnes. The three other men, which made the total number to be seven, were each holding an animal, or totem, captive. One was a large, black-and-gray mottled wolf, on a silver chain, who was baying rather ferociously at us. The second was the crow, named Lizhini, that the medicine man had used in Mrs. Gordon's courtroom drama and to frighten Penelope. The last animal was the coyote, named First Angry, that had been used to trick Miss Farmer and to fool us while we were inside our mansions, and even at the Fourth of July picnic, when Ajei had counterfeited her illness so as to be transported to the public hospital.

"This is the wolf and the skinwalker in one," the medicine man explained to us, smiling for the first time I had seen him do so. There are no wild and stalking creatures, as is being discussed in the other newspapers and magazines. There are no raving medicine men out to take your lives. There is simply this well-trained and ravenous species of wolf, who is as innocent of guilt as Penelope Farmer is.

There you have my story, friends. The last dark layers of my onion have been peeled away for your inspection. Each of our ten captives shall return to your society because we were never meant to be fooled, this time around. Captain Lees had contrived to have the Bureau of Indian Affairs Police, together with the Colorado State Police, there at the scene, and they rescued us that same morning of July 13th.

My mother, your publisher, will circulate many more excellent articles than this one, I am very certain. They may even contain the detailed action you crave, to arouse your senses, and to keep you alert to the evil in mankind one more day. They may not even contain the truth, such as the response mother received to her editorial in this newspaper about the persecution of the Navajo on the reservation. That response was written by Mrs. Crutchfield to lure us away from suspecting her.

If there are deaths from vigilante justice, or from people who believe the untruths being published by our competitors, then I must remind you of the nature of journalistic sources. We ten were the only ones who were there. My mother and Captain Lees were the only people there who knew the underlying truth. My mother may offend you with her suffragist sympathies and her indelicate forth rightfulness, but she will always try her utmost to be honest with you. I will stay in San Francisco, as she moves down to San Diego, but she will remain in my mind and in my heart.

The famous "Scarlet Sisters" from England, Victoria and Tennessee Claflin, have agreed to support and to help my mother with her variety of causes, especially the one that concerns establishing a Public Defender's Office in the State of California. My mother's oldest son, and my brother, Samuel Cortland Foltz, will also remain in San Francisco to be with his bride-to-be, Adeline Quantrill. Mother has promised to ride the train up for the wedding. Our family's best friend, Ah Toy, will continue her art and her investments in Nob Hill and San Jose, and we shall see her anon. Alas, the love of my mother's later life, Captain Isaiah Lees, will be staying in San Francisco as well. As for Dr. Andrew McFarland, he will return to his duties at his private sanitarium in Illinois, but he will remain a close friend and expert witness when mother and Mrs. Gordon need an alienist to verify the mental competency of a client on trial. And mother's grand onion-peeling partner, Attorney Laura de Force Gordon, shall be defending the weak from the powerful, giving love to whomever she finds worthy of such love, and speaking out for all of the defenseless people in our great and ever-evolving society.

I hope you can find your own layers of onion to peel away. Remember, please understand we all have subjective onions of our own choosing; but the bigger onion, which all societies, religions, and genders call "Earth," does not need us to find the collective Truth. For she is the Mother of all Truths, and we are her gracious guests, and we must, to survive, treat her with the utmost respect and husbandry that goes beyond selfish ends, and into future generations of our living progeny, no matter how they may come into this world.

Next Mystery, *Stingaree*, in the Portia of the Pacific Historical Mystery series.

The "Stingaree" was the Red-Light District of San Diego in the late 1880s. This novel will take place in 1888. Attorney Clara Foltz moves to San Diego with two of her children, and some of the other historical characters in this novel are Dr. Charlotte Baker, the first female medical physician in San Diego, Josephine Sarah "Sadie" Marcus, Wyatt Earp's common law wife, and Ida Bailey, the infamous Madame of one of San Diego's "high class" bordellos, the Canary Cottage.

At the heart of my new murder mystery *Stingaree* is a bare-knuckle competition arranged by Wyatt Earp. He markets it as "The Hundred-Round Fight," even though it lasts only four. It also features a cock fight, a bull fight, and a preliminary match.

Stingaree

Chapter 1: The Hundred-Round Fight

Tijuana, Mexico, May 6, 1888.

Ida

Thank you, Mrs. Foltz, for allowing me to describe what happened that day. However, because of the phantom nature of my thoughts, I cannot vouch for the authenticity of what I experienced. Your daughter, Bertha May, appears pleasant enough. She squints a bit when she writes, so you may want to have her vision examined. You have guaranteed that what I tell you will not be given to the newspapers or to other press sources. This testimony of mine is for legal purposes only. I understand. Your job as the defense attorney is to gather testimony of eyewitnesses to this murder. My testimony is being used by the prosecution as well? I see. There were four of us who saw this murder being committed? Can you tell me the others' names? We shall surely meet if we are called into court. In fact, I probably already know them. Believe it or not, I am quite the society gadfly, despite the nature of my occupation.

Josephine Marcus? Of course. I do know her very well. We have self-same interests, although she never likes to admit her past experiences in my line of endeavor. I understand. Sadie's common law husband, Wyatt Earp, is your client, the accused. I did not realize Sadie was there, actually, because I was under the influence at the time. Mr. Elias Baldwin? Lucky! I also know him. He gambles quite a bit, and he has visited my cottage upon several occasions. I understand he knows Wyatt quite well, as they are both investing in our real estate boom. I do recall seeing him on the night of the big boxing event in Tijuana. It was before I took the drug. He had purchased one of my lovely escorts, Marie, for the evening. Did either of these two know Mr. Sonenschein, the victim? I am so sorry. I have a very inquisitive nature, as you shall see. Who is the third fellow witness? You? You must be in jest. I see. You were there reporting the event for your newspaper. That is quite understandable. Why did I not see you, I wonder? You were where? Up in a tree overlooking the arena? You also had a box camera? Quite ingenious. I can understand that. There were many other journalists trying to get photographs, and you decided to take to the trees like our monkey relatives! We women must be especially daring to compete, do we not? Of course, I shall continue my narrative now.

I must stipulate at the outset that much of what I shall describe to you shall be of an internal variety. It is the nature of mescaline, the hallucinogenic ingredient contained in the peyote cactus, to give the user a way to appreciate the common interdependence of living beings and not their antagonisms, which are usually caused by the ones in control of the social rules and obligations.

On that day, my vision, both externally at the scene around me, and internally, at the comparisons I was making in my mind, was acutely attentive due to my ingesting the cactus buttons, peyote. My self-importance and cultural identities began to melt from my body. I became a cyclops, and my all-consuming spiritual power made me see things around me as if I were the microscopic lens of that part of me, which is connected to you all, and my attention was held rapt simply by my being close to the object in my purview.

If you have already placed me in a negative category of your mind, I understand. I warrant that not many in my profession of harlotry have vocabularies as advanced as my own, and not many have studied books in the library as frequently as I have. When you are born without papers, orphaned by the mother who gave you life, you begin to experience the reality of living inside the world of poverty. The vow you make to yourself is that you will never experience such mental depravity and physical squalor again, if you can prevent it. The first escape route I saw was to be able to mimic the grand community leaders who would visit Our Lady of Guadalupe Catholic Mission Orphanage on Fifth Avenue. A large vocabulary was at the top of my list.

The male benefactors, many of whom would gaze down at us girls, had glittering, pale-colored eyes darting in their sockets. Their eyes were like Mrs. Ortega's, when she would read to us about Little Red Riding Hood's grandmother in bed. "Oh, Grandmother. What big eyes you have! exclaimed Red."

Even though these men had wolfish eyes, I eventually learned how they spoke, and what they found important, so I could convince them to pay attention to me. I was no longer simply in the genus of orphan and species of female human, required to gather around their legs like a reverent doll, a prayer of thanks on my lips, ready to bow and curtsy for their favors. I was Ida Bailey, the little red-haired riding hood pursuing the wolf. I wanted to avenge my literary grandmother, whom I envisioned was held captive inside their full bellies.

My imaginary grandmother, as I knew her, had no hereditary lineage to trap one inside a traditional family way of life. As I viewed these outdated kinds of women, they were raised to become subservient and fashionable powder puffs out in society. However, at home, they were kept as a functional ovulating machine, ready to procreate at the whim of their lord and master. They kept the home free of dirt, grime, and grit, tending to the daily chores of "mother," which was a job invented by men to trap their women inside a dangerous wheel of torture and pain, with little or no time for what these women really desired.

My grandmother was billions of years old, who had, as in Darwin's *Origin of the Species*, evolved from the same tribes of monkeys and apes that first appeared in this magnificent Garden of Earthly Delights. More than that. My grandmother taught me I was born from the stars above, as were all of us, and the only power I needed was from the sun. I looked around me at this world I was inhabiting, and I knew I had come from a time and a place that knew no boundaries or restrictions imposed from the outside. My origins allowed complete freedom on the inside. The memories which were poured into one's brain by the institutions were not the source of real knowledge. Real understanding takes place after the human mind has been freed from all interference caused by the selfish social realm into which one is born. The power from the stars is enough to allow the unconstrained mind to channel the full radiance of true freedom.

From the women's magazines, in the San Diego Library's reference section, I was learning which dress to drape upon my developing body, and what words to speak to woo the male stargazers. I knew my glow of freed intelligence must appear alluring to these tall men who wielded so much power. They had candies and coins in their pockets. They could whistle and sing, play harmonicas, and even dance jigs! They, who smelled of European linen and the best cologne, smoked long cigars from Cuba, and drank bottled water from artesian wells. They owned the key to the door of Our Lady of Guadalupe and to my personal salvation.

I was, in my post as Madam of the Canary Cottage, Horatia, the female version of Hamlet's best friend. Instead of dying in a tragic duel, I won, by teaching Hamlet how to dance with his father's ghost instead of fearing him and going murderously mad. I taught these important men how to truly enjoy us, their women of leisure.

We, who catered to their every fantasy, their every carnal desire, were the same women who laughed and pointed at the passing lines of Suffragettes on Broadway, demonstrating for equality, not understanding that it was not an equal that men desired but a reflector of their own greatness.

They knew their wives were pliant and submissive, creating a concern over family matters. I and my ladies, in counter response, became fussy about *them*. We learned to dress in opera gowns, smoke from long Parisian cigarette holders, drink champagne from our corsets, dance on velvet red table cloths, our bodies revolving under the spinning, multi-colored overhead chandelier. The band played *Dreamland*: "Down upon the silent waters, floating on the crystal stream ..." as we danced for our breakfasts, lunches, and dinners, at the best restaurants in town.

Riding in private black carriages, the windows tinted black, these important men pulled up to my Canary Cottage, or, depending on their intoxication, to other San Diego Stingaree houses of ill repute. Except our Canary fantasy dreamland gave us access to their bodies and their minds, and this is where the fun really begins, isn't it, ladies and gentlemen? According to my Fairy Grandmother, who was living inside these wolfish men, who had devoured her long ago, I am billions of years in the making. I can channel pure energy, so what I say and do break the boundaries of time and space. A completely free mind is the direct source of eternal light, whose waves of flowing atoms transform into physical shapes, on the way toward the first stimuli of infinitesimal life forms.

The men who came to my Canary Cottage knew I provided what they needed to fulfill themselves as real men. To be completely forthcoming, I also provided "special real men" to some of these real men. And, yes, this is still the Wild West, as the Penny Press likes to call it, and we cater to any fancy. Women seeking women. Men seeking men. I stop at children and at animals. Why? Not because of the Bible or other holy text. I stop because, since ancient times, children and animals have been protected from outside harm. Until recently, in our part of the world, if you stole a person's horse, you could be put to death. And children, according to the Romantics, have come from the angelic spheres, so their innocence must be kept intact until their minds can determine a personal identity.

Our young children, and the animals they imitate in games, pantomimes, and stories, should never be used for any carnal or capital purpose. True. This is not the rule the world over, as different habits and customs can become completely unique inside each of our brains. The grave mistake, I know, comes about when these thoughts become laws, and the corrupt group's adherents grow in number, and loyalty to cultural values and laws eventually controls their minds. The society establishes the rules, and they are repeated every day, in the schools, in the bedrooms, in the boardrooms, until these rules are second nature. Dr. Freud of Austria, according to Rabbi Sonenschein, calls it the "unconscious," deep inside the brain. The unconscious rules the conscious, and is many times greater, as it is a repository for all the billions of sensory impressions we receive every day. Whereas, if each brain could remain pure and free from these societal pressures, then the pure love energy of intelligent purpose might become our collective salvation because it obliterates these strict rules of convention and replaces it with Eros, sensual freedom.

I believe it is this love energy of intelligent purpose that keeps me yearning for each day to begin again. Perhaps men like Secretary and Chief Special Agent of the New York Society for the Suppression of Vice … What was that you said, Mrs. Foltz? And Post Office Inspector? Quite right. The fact is, men do not simply enjoy largesse in their affairs, including their status titles, they also enjoy women who can feed them their fantasies of lust one delicious tidbit at a time, one exhilarating moment at a time. These men want an unlimited expansion of the senses. My women and I are what I like to term "Traps for young men" and their unconscious cravings. For, you see, my ideas for creating my Canary Cottage came from the pages of this little book, with the same title, written by Sodom and Gomorrah's Postal Inspector, Archangel from Heaven, and dry goods salesman on Earth, Mr. Anthony Comstock.

As you know, Attorney Foltz, I am only one of your four eyewitnesses. I am also probably the least valuable to your investigation. As we have discussed at length, on the day and location of the murder in Tijuana, wherein we have now returned, I was under the influence of the two Peyote buttons which symbolize, to me, my ancient Grandmother's eyes. This means that when I did my belly dance what I saw was streaming directly from the pure energy of our Creator, Preserver, and Destroyer, the *Ein Sof.*

What I shall describe will not be understood by normal readers educated in the prison schools of American society. Although, perhaps a few might be able to puncture the veil of my symbolism. As some readers of Mr. Carroll's *Through the Looking-Glass* know so well, the phantom Alice inside the mirror is also a part of the human Alice standing in front of the mirror. As I will demonstrate, Alice merely needs to believe in her own magical ideas in order to step through the mirror to make them real. Even though the magical world of uniqueness makes your surroundings strange, the ultimate freedom it gives you is worth the temporary maladjustments.

After I read Mr. Comstock's book, what I saw were not chapters filled with "thou shall nots." Instead, I created my own version of "thou shall," from my Fairy Grandmother's imagination. These ideas were certainly not coming from my old life, as I was seen by most San Diego citizens as a poverty-stricken maiden, who, except for the transient beauty and impetuous nature of a wild red vixen, was condemned forever to struggle within a menial existence.

Of course, that was until I read about Mr. Comstock. This gentleman protector of virtue, my Walrus Prophet, and his little book of "shall nots," gave me the very personal pattern I needed to seek my vein of golden providence in California. The fact that he was also witness to this murder is neither here nor there. Having read about Mr. Wyatt Earp's "Hundred-Round Fight" in your newspaper, *The San Diego Daily Bee*, Mr. Comstock was here to entrap me and my clients in one of his clever artifices. I am certain he will have his own tale to impart, so I shall not muddy the waters of your investigation with my own prejudices against the man. You must be aware that he does figure into my description of what I witnessed. You, as a journalist and lawyer, must surely understand the impossibility of being completely unbiased when using fickle symbols such as words. It is your job to put together these different viewpoints in order to arrive at the truth, is it not?

Grand Jury, you say? I understand. These are upstanding members of our San Diego community who are charged with determining whether there are enough tangible evidence and unbiased witnesses presented to bring an accused to trial for First Degree Murder. No, I am not familiar with the role of a witness. There has been only one murder committed in my place of business, and I was not in the room when it occurred. Yes, the murderess was the wife of one of my clients, who came searching for her husband one evening at the behest of her four children. That was *her* excuse, of course. I, as the proprietress of the Canary Cottage, do not ask my clients about their personal and familial relations. Why should I? I create a fantasy world, like Alice's Wonderland. In fact, I inform each of my employees, whether man or woman, that he or she is charged with granting wishes that make each client the happiest. These clients come to us because they cannot, for one private reason or another, fulfill these wishes elsewhere in society.

I see. You have your own experience with brothels. Miss Ah Toy in San Francisco. You represented her as an attorney? I know this is neither the time nor place, but I would certainly enjoy speaking privately with you about your experiences. Perhaps at a later date? Very well. I shall continue.

I realize another lie. There were five witnesses to this murder instead of four, as you told me previously. Oh. I can now see more deeply. It was, you believe, Mr. Comstock's secret fantasy that set-in motion the events leading to the murder of the Jewish Mystic, and itinerant, Jerome Sonenschein. He is why there became five witnesses. The fifth witness, however, is an antagonist of at least one of the other eye witnesses. How many more tentacles of negative energy were there between these linchpins of justice and their societal prey, you ask? These are the heady questions only you can answer, Mrs. Foltz. Call you Clara? Very well, I shall.

What I observed that night was a phantasmagorical vision. I did not know I was seeing someone being murdered. To me, as you will soon realize, as did I, the evening was divided in two halves. The first half, when I came to the party before the main event, what Wyatt Earp had billed as the "100-round Fight," I was checking on my four girls and one young man, who were contracted to work that night as escorts for privileged clients. They first saw my employees when I took my Canary Cottage bandwagon out for a spin down Broadway, along the business mile of banks, saloons, restaurants, and hotels.

The men knew my business plan. Each woman and one man wore a different color: red, green, blue, yellow, and brown. The first client to bring a poker chip of that color to me at the Canary Cottage could take my employee to the big extravaganza across the border into Mexico. Yes, Clara, I was also part of the main attraction, and this was how I came to make the acquaintance of the victim, Rabbi Jerome Sonenschein. He was the immigrant who journeyed from Brody, in the Ukraine, where his people were being persecuted by Austrians, on one side of their border, and Russians on the other. His city had lost its status as a tax-free commercial hub, in 1879, and was being taxed. Not only that, the Rabbi told me, upon our first meeting, but his own Jewish brethren, who made up eighty-eight percent of Brody's population, had turned against his Kabballah teachings and marked him as a "blasphemer and idolater." They believed his strange teachings had turned the Russians and Austrians against them.

The rabbi came to New York City by boat, not a penny to his name. From there, he joined a caravan of settlers traveling to California, and he settled in San Diego, after roaming for weeks with a contingent of Mormons, who were sympathetic to his plight, and who thought of themselves as one of the "lost tribes of Israel." When he heard that some also practiced polygamy, he believed he had indeed discovered a long-lost tribe of brethren.

I spent the spring studying with Rabbi Sonenschein. I remember because my ladies had ventured up into the Anza-Borrego desert to harvest wild flowers for our cottage. Come to think of it, rabbi called my workers and I human wild flowers, and the rains that were so necessary to the desert blossoms' growth applied to us as well in the form of real estate storm's excesses. These land speculators and builders were our best clients, as they were to all of San Diego, yet we in the flesh and spirit trade had to capture their viscera before we could allow them to use our outsides for their pleasures.

Yes, I'm coming to that. Rabbi Sonenschein explained to me that his religion was based on his ability to see through the seven veils which cover us from the Divine Light, the *Ein Sof*. He always wore the same suit, an old black frock, similar to those worn by priests in the missions. But on the surface of this long frock, and also etched upon the round *kippah* on his head, were hundreds of letters and numbers of many languages, fonts and sizes. When I asked him what they were, he went into what I was later to learn was his deepest meditative unconsciousness. His lips moved under his black beard and riveting, yet staring raven eyes. I am able to hear his words any night when I'm alone, and the sounds of the nocturnal carnal escapades have finally disappeared. There is only me and his words, whispering, the letters taking form, dancing in the light of the window where the stars poured in their luminescence.

"Behind the seventh veil of the world's illusion lies a direct connection with the infinite mind of our Creator. My coat is an attempt to capture the name of this Creator in symbolic form to allow us to contemplate it and to realize it. This is possible if one has lost consciousness completely and can follow this Creator's instructions down to the last detail."

I am an intelligent young woman, Clara. I must admit, however, that I had no inkling as to what this mystic was telling me. What of these seven veils? I knew of Salomé, the Jewess stepdaughter of Herod Antipas, and her stepmother Herodias. Salomé's mother was Mariamne, the daughter of Simon, the Jewish high priest. Herodias took offence when John the Baptist, the prophet, said she was disobeying God's law. She had married her husband Philips's brother, Herod Antipas, while Philip was still alive. Herod, on his birthday, wanted to see Salomé dance her specialty number wearing the seven veils.

Each veil, in its seductive order, was removed by her, as she swirled and leaped in front of the campfire to please the king and his entourage of nobles. When I told the rabbi about this, he laughed. He said behind her last veil was the Truth of the Divine Light. It was not carnal pleasure, as many philosophers believed, and it was not some passage into the hell of temptation, lust, and murder. For, as we know, the biblical Salomé had promised her mother the head from John the Baptist, who had insulted her marriage to the king. Herodias convinced Salomé to tell her husband she would dance for him at his palace revelry. In return, the king must cut the head from the false prophet John's shoulders and bring it to Herodias.

Now, I shall enumerate the explanation he gave me, which eventually evolved into the horrendous murder of the rabbi in Mexico. Many artists and philosophers of the Enlightenment were sympathetic to the dancer, Salomé. Herodias was an evil witch to force this impressionable and artistic young woman into doing what she did. Salomé was completely innocent, and her stepmother was to blame.

But then, in our present Romantic Era, the same assortment of literary and philosophical experts changed their minds. It was the time when each person was believed to have a unique and completely free will. Therefore, the Jewess could have refused her mother. She could have been courageous and stood up to her insulted parent. Instead, Salomé disobeyed her moral compass, which was controlled by Jewish law, and she danced a most wickedly vile and magical enchantment that cost John the Baptist his head.

At this moment, the rabbi grabbed me by my shoulders so abruptly that my head wobbled. His black pupils were slightly enlarged but were riveted in a concentrated stare into my own windows of the soul. He explained the symbolism of each veil Salomé used in her dance, as it corresponded to his doctrine of finding what he called "The Zohar," the Divine Light of the Creator, Preserver, and Destroyer of this mystical realm. He said this dominion became illuminated once this final cataract veil was lifted from our eyes.

His words are also marked upon my brain as the Ten

Commandments were marked upon the stone tablets by Yahweh, the unnameable. I shall always remember them. Especially now that the rabbi is dead. Before I began my dance that night here in Mexico, before I took my drug, Rabbi Sonenschein explained my purpose.

He told me the first veil I must cast off allowed the meditators upon my body to begin to work in the wisdom of internality, which is sweeter than honey and nectar, opens the eyes, and revives the soul. It allows you to find a hidden delight, sweet as the light to the eyes, and good for the soul, refining and illuminating your brain with good and upright qualities, tasting the flavor of the hidden Light of the next world in this world through the wisdom of *The Zohar*.

The second veil that I must loosen from around my undulating form, and allow to drift away on the evening's breeze, allowed viewers to feel the light and the future reward within their bodies. Their flesh would begin to tingle, their loins begin to moisten, and their brains would become infused with my brain. Their faces would come alive with new radiance and with an appreciation of all that was around them was infinite.

My third veil would be difficult. It must remain around my body the longest, clinging with static energy that seems to be welded to me in a most diabolical manner. I will curse and spit upon it, and still it clings, like the first man who raped me in the orphanage, his orange body hair shaking particles of some secret earth mineral upon my nakedness. He had been digging for his fortune deep inside a hellish mine. Once I am able to repel the third veil, it will disintegrate, with a flash of lightning, and the viewers will be able to view the false façades worn by all humans in this dark world of trickery, shadows, and light. Their insight into character and mental cruelties will be rejuvenating and will satisfy their urge to become omniscient and yet they will still cling to the passions of this life. There were three more veils to destroy before the ultimate goal was attained, he reminded me.

The rabbi's voice now sounds raspy in my mind. For it is not me, nor is it my subconscious brain which now remembers his instructions. No, it is his voice and his brain, even from the land of

Sheol, of Forgetfulness and Death, which make me confess to you once more.

I was ordered by him to dance into the fourth realm in a circular spiral towards the infinite Seventh Seal veil, in the white-hot center core of my being. He said I would suddenly hear a female voice from outside my meditative cocoon. Are you not aware, voice, that female-loving men, when shown photographs of women, of similar beauty, will always select the ones whose pupils have been enlarged by mydriasis drugs? Such as mescaline. This was what I used in my own dance that night, voice. Voice? You are Clara Foltz, the attorney? Oh, there you are, and your lovely daughter, Bertha May.

The fourth veil I would cast off gave the audience a vision of the magnitude of the Creator's Dominion. Planetary solar systems would fill the sky in their minds. It was a moving, rolling tapestry that never stopped whirling, pulsing outward and then pulling inward once more. Expanding and constricting, spiraling galaxies, streaking comets, and exploding stars. To my audience, my legs would be seen moving beneath my final three veils. I was that vision of loveliness conditioned by billions of my sisters of the past, who, over the millennia, had learned to harness nature's neurological Eden to give dancers like me power over these hunter males.

Rabbi Sonenschein, the mystic, told me the gender of the dancer and watcher means nothing. Male watching female. Male watching male. Female watching male. Female watching female. It was the symbolism of what was behind these veils that was important, not the lust the dance might provoke in the heat of the moment. Although lust *was* a part of my appeal, at the beginning, he explained that the purpose of my dance was to transfix and reveal a deeper meaning to them. Men were usually much larger, much more conditioned by pain and their chosen role as tribal protectors. The continuing passage of infinite galactic possibilities, caused by shedding the fourth veil, will make my mouth water from thirst. I will know I still had to continue to dance for three more rounds, and my body will begin to sweat, the beads forming on the surface of my arms, legs, and torso like droplets on desert sands.

The fifth veil, he said, would create a frozen moment in time and space. Each of my observers would be able to fantasize whatever it was made them happiest. It was as if the prospect of reaching the seventh veil made a fissure which created a dream within the mind that was not controlled by one's chronological age. Instead, the reality of seeing this thin, red piece of silk brush against my skin for the last time was a passageway to a moment of existential joy beyond the usual pain and suffering of the world's dramas. He said, if I watched them carefully, I would be able to notice a smile on each of their faces. It might be caused by a childhood toy, or the first kiss during a spring shower. No matter what the moment was, it would suspend the viewer in a wonderful rapture. After I cast it aside, the person who caught this veil would be able to have the first wish he or she made come true.

I understand, Clara. That is a good description of what I was experiencing. I felt like I was in *A Thousand and One Arabian Nights*. Now that a murder has been committed, I wish I could go back in time and tell the rabbi I could not dance for him. Wait one moment. I don't remember. Did Shahrazad survive her ordeal of telling stories to the king? Yes? Thank you, little miss. I suppose there is hope for me yet.

I am not speaking too quickly for you to copy, am I, Bertha May? Does your mother employ you in her business quite often? You once pretended to be mad inside the Stockton State Insane Asylum? How exciting for you! I hope you won your case. I see. This story of mine is also becoming quite extended. Only two more veils, and then I can tell you what happened after I took the mescaline.

I know as I reach the final veil, the reality of what happened while I was dancing was not in the realm of sensory perception. That is why I am attempting to explain the meaning of each according to the victim. When I tell you what I saw when I was hallucinating under the control of the drug, you will be able to compare and contrast these details with what your other witnesses experienced. I must emphasize the fact that it was my choice to take mescaline and not Rabbi Sonenschein's. The fifth veil diverged most from what he told me would happen.

I understand your analogy very well, Clara. Finding the truth is quite like peeling the layers from an onion. I shall now explain what I saw from the perspective of my state of hallucination while dancing to reveal the fifth, sixth and seventh veils. I understand. The rabbi was shot during the reveal of the seventh veil, and I was also quite naked. Can you now understand why I believe my testimony may not be valuable to you? I was in the center of the onion, which, of course, has no center. Be prepared to set your sacred Suffrage Movement back at least two thousand years.

Now I begin.

STINGAREE

Historical Notes

In my present society, which features extreme views of a social and political nature, I wanted to write a mystery novel that depicted the harm of this "fake news," for want of a better term. For, you see, I believe the same social problems exist, no matter what the chronological era. In the late 1880s, when this novel is set, most of journalism was depicting our activities through words, and, very infrequently, through images. As a professor of English for over twenty years, I know that words are the most psychologically problematic tools to describe what is real. Even today, with almost every sensory communication tool available to our reporters, we still are being controlled by the underlying realities of capitalistic, communistic, and despotic greed, political power-mongers, and cliques of terrorist opportunists.

However, today, when the violent consequences of this phenomena can happen in the blink of a camera's eye, back then it took much longer for the result to be seen on the many thousands of pages of news print in the late 1880s. Therefore, when one writes about this era, one must understand that it is rather like attempting to write inside a vat of molasses. I am rather fond, as you have seen, of metaphor. I first learned of the "onion as reality" metaphor when I was getting "clean and sober." The image has stayed in my consciousness all these sober years now, and I have finally been able to use it!

Sometimes, even today, it takes events a long time to percolate and to brew into a heady froth of that "aha moment," which enters my brain, to finally inspire me. The present movement toward making the choice of abortion illegal, once again, was the impetus for this novel. However, a woman's choice to abort her fetus merely serves as a metaphor for the wider issue of those who get condemned because of their economic, cultural, and psychological needs.

I do want to separate historical reality from my fictional dream world. I will not give elaborate explanations concerning characteristics, except when I believe it is warranted by historical

177

fact. All of the characters portrayed in this novel are based on real people except for seven, and my projected reality of the eighth person, who was real, is so fictionalized as to make him a complete fabrication.

Here are the seven fictional characters: 1. Penelope Farmer. 2. Haseya Farmer. 3. Aloysius Farmer. 4. Ajei. 5. Mr. Edward Barnes. 6. Mrs. Althea Crutchfield. 7. Judge Frederick Lattimore. The eighth character is Hástin Yázhe, who is based on an actual Navajo medicine man of the 1800s, but whose character is completely fictionalized.

My main characters in the Portia of the Pacific series are still intact. Mrs. Clara Shortridge Foltz is moving down to San Diego, at long last, in the next book. She also did this in her real life. I live here, so I am excited to do the requisite research to portray my home environs appropriately. Her daughter, Trella Evelyn, who was an actress in her life, was close to my writer's heart as I portrayed her in this story. Although her activities inside this novel are fiction, I hope I was able to capture her artist's soul.

There was some controversy surrounding my portrayal of Clara's friend and fellow attorney, Laura de Force Gordon. I used the actual historical inscription left in a non-fiction book, which Laura wrote and included in a San Francisco time capsule, to base my theory that she was probably a lover of the same sex. It causes her quite a problem in this plot, and it is important to the complete evolution of my theme. There were no #metoo movements or LBGTQ rights in 1887. When one was "outed," the consequences could be far worse on the person than it is today, but the emotional issue is still the same. Do we recognize the underlying desires the person faces, or do we lump them in with some religious or societal prejudice based on fear and misunderstanding?

In fact, indigenous peoples were much more gender fluid than their overlords. Many tribes have complex language to include multiple genders and sexualities. While each tribe has its own unique terminology, "two spirit" has become the term to denote a Native American who feels he or she has multiple genders within him or her. Maintaining these traditions was very difficult during the

1800-1900s due to the dynamics occurring in Victorian society being imposed through colonization. Many of these people were violently forced to assimilate by missionaries, boarding schools, and the U.S. Government.

My great-great-grandmother on my mother's side was a Mi'kmaq tribal member from the Canadian Provence of Nova Scotia. The question of Native American rights is literally running through my veins. Although my villains are Navajo, I hope the reader can see past the fiction enough to appreciate the deeper meaning. My enjoyment of the late Tony Hillerman's novels about Navajo life, Skinwalkers, and my own research into their history, gave me a new understanding about our Great Plains Natives and the discrimination and horrors they faced and are still facing today.

When Prosecutor Vincent Bugliosi was able to prove that Charles Manson used drugs, sex, intimidation, and fear to control his "family" and was therefore responsible for the Tate-Labianca murders, without physically harming anyone, it set a precedent. Penelope Farmer, in this novel, was a victim of the same kind of drug, sex, and mind-control techniques, but it happened in 1887, rather than 1969. If my reader is so offended in 2019 by reading about a victim of such mind-control, then he or she is not paying attention to what is going on around us. In many ways, we are becoming victims of a similar brand of mind-control, in the media, and by rapists and pedophiles like Jeffrey Epstein, and even by our own leaders.

I also used the Scarlet Sisters, Victoria and Tennessee Claflin, and I hope I captured their authenticity and love for the spiritual side of life and their defense of women's rights and the plight of the poor and downtrodden. I also tried to point out their foibles. They deserve novels based on their characters, and I hope they've been written or are going to be written.

I enjoyed researching the legal scholarship of former Chief Justice of the United States Supreme Court, Oliver Wendell Holmes, Junior. Bringing him into the courtroom was quite a joy for me to experience, and I hope you got a kick out of it as well. I worked for a law school for ten years, and although I never became a lawyer, I was fascinated by the law and the lawyers who practiced. I hope that fascination carried over into my fiction.

On the Prosecution's side, I included Dr. Horatio Storer, who led the campaign which resulted in making abortion illegal in the United States. His writings and "philosophy" are still used by today's Pro-Life Movement, and the issue of abortion is continuing into the Twenty-First Century.

Finally, when Trella Evelyn's editorial hit the streets of San Diego, I envisioned my small town of ranchers, townspeople, Mexican-Americans, and Chinese immigrants reading it and appreciating the fact that they were getting a "true" version of what happened that day at Four Corners. It is my contention, to this day, that those who understand the basic logic behind legal and journalism research, which says that the best sources are the people who directly experience the event, will understand the problems we face today in the media. The fact of the matter is, people are judging others by information they see on Facebook and other social media based on second-hand duplicity and innuendo. When Clara travels south to San Diego, she shall be taking her love of natural truth with her. I hope you enjoy her further legal and detective adventures as much as I will enjoy creating them for her—and for you.

Please join our social page to ask questions of the author.
Facebook.com/portiaofpacific/

About the Author

James Musgrave's work has been recently featured in *Best New Writing 2011*, Eric Hoffer Book Awards, Hopewell Press, Titusville, N.J. He was semi-finalist in the Black River Chapbook Competition, Fall, 2012. He was also in a Bram Stoker Award Finalist volume of horror fiction, *Beneath the Surface, 13 Shocking Tales of Terror*, Shroud Publishing, San Francisco, CA. His historical mystery series starring Detective Patrick James O'Malley was selected as "featured titles" by the American Library Association's Self-E Program for Independent Authors. The first mystery in that series, *Forevermore*, won the First-Place blue ribbon for Best Historical Mystery, in the Chanticleer International Clue Book Awards, 2013. James lives in San Diego, and is the publisher of EMRE Publishing, LLC.

Sign-up for the Author's Newsletter at emrepublishing.com